She could barely control herself...

"If all the gentlemen in London are as rude as you, my lord," Alyssa said, "then perhaps I would be happier staying in the country. But before long, sir, whether you think it likely or not, the Wentworths will appear at Almack's and anywhere else that your kind are welcome."

To her complete embarrassment, Lord Brookmere only laughed. "Very well, Miss Wentworth. Almack's it is, but pray don't forget to save a dance for me—perhaps a waltz? I'm sure a young lady of your ingenuity would find a way not only to get vouchers but to obtain permission to waltz, as well. Good day."

A HINT
OF SCANDAL
ALBERTA SINCLAIR

Harlequin Books

TORONTO • NEW YORK • LONDON
AMSTERDAM • PARIS • SYDNEY • HAMBURG
STOCKHOLM • ATHENS • TOKYO • MILAN

To the memory of Rose Corino,
who introduced me to the joy of reading romances

Published March 1987
ISBN 0-373-31015-3

CHAPTER ONE

"ALYSSA, DEAREST, do you think that I would look a *complete* quiz in that hat?" Miss Henrietta Wentworth considered a dainty creation of chip straw and cherry silk displayed to great advantage in a milliner's window.

"Perhaps it is a shade too dashing for such a wizened old thing as I!" She giggled and shot an arch look at her niece. "Though I daresay no one would guess I was turned forty already if I appeared in such a getup!"

Miss Alyssa Wentworth, a petite, golden-haired young lady of half her aunt's years was gazing with thoughtful green eyes at an impressive turnout that had just drawn up in the inn yard across the way. She tore her glance away with difficulty.

"I—I'm sorry, Aunt Henrietta. I'm afraid I wasn't attending..." She turned back to the display of hats, but her full, coral pink lips were pursed in speculation. It was not often that a sporting curricle with four splendid matched bays, driven by a tall, handsome man in a smart caped driving coat and yellow gloves, visited such a dull place as Swinbury.

Hoping to distract her aunt's attention from this interesting scene, which she knew would send the little lady into the most inconvenient raptures, she remarked on a very ugly satin-straw bonnet in the corner of the window, but it was too late. Her niece's inattention had awakened Miss Wentworth's curiosity, and as she turned to watch the gentleman step down from his curricle, her eyes widened with admiration.

"Oh, my love, only look—see how fine that carriage is!"

Alyssa cringed at her aunt's shrill tones, sure to be heard by the driver of the object of their praise. She quietly urged the older lady to lower her voice.

"But, why, dearest?" asked the indefatigable Henrietta. "I'm sure it is no fault of mine if that is the handsomest curricle I've ever seen. And what a fine gentleman drives it! Why, his coat alone must have cost twenty guineas."

Never before had Alyssa been so conscious or so ashamed of her aunt's sometimes vulgar peculiarities. Nor was she to be saved further embarrassment, for the owner of the coat had obviously heard these words. He turned and fixed them with so cool and arrogant a stare that she wished the earth would open and swallow her. Henrietta, however, saw nothing amiss, and gave the gentleman a little wave and a simper.

"Lord, he quite puts me in mind of Colonel Bowles, who was forever calling on me in Bath. He was of just such a height and with just such a fine leg as that gentleman yonder."

She chattered on, deaf to all entreaties, while Alyssa was sure that she could feel the gentleman's indignant stare burning a hole in the back of her russet pelisse. She ventured to peep over her shoulder, and instantly regretted it, for to her extreme mortification the gentleman was scrutinizing them through a quizzing glass, disgust plainly written on his elegant countenance. She looked away quickly, and took her aunt's arm to lead her down the street.

Just as Alyssa was congratulating herself on having escaped from the scene of her embarrassment, Henrietta caught sight of a display of muslins in the window of a shop opposite, only yards away from the inn where the stranger now stood conferring with his two servants.

"Come, Alyssa, I want to look over those new goods in Brewer's shop. Madame Louise must make up some lavender muslin for my half mourning."

With this she darted across the way, blithely ignoring the shouts of a carter and the local doctor in his gig as she passed within inches of a huge draft horse and heavy wagon. By the time Alyssa had crossed the street after her it was too late to prevent her from addressing an unsolicited greeting to the gentleman who had excited her admiration.

Alyssa watched in deep chagrin as her aunt was icily rebuffed with the merest inclination of the head and a forbidding glance before the gentleman turned away.

"Oh, well, I am sure I did not mean any harm...." Henrietta stood staring after him as her niece took her arm, and Alyssa saw that her brown eyes brimmed with tears. Anger overcame embarrassment at the insolence of a gentleman who presumed to insult a simple and good-natured soul like Henrietta Wentworth.

"Never mind him, my dear," she said gently. "Why don't you go in and look at those muslins? I will join you shortly." She left her aunt in the shop, and without knowing precisely what she meant to do, turned toward the offending personage, just in time to hear him speak to his manservant.

"I fear, Mallow, that if females of that sort are representative of the society to be met with here, my friend will soon be regretting his intention to settle in this neighborhood."

The spark of anger that his snub had ignited in Alyssa's breast was as nothing to the blaze that burned there now. With vengeance in mind, she followed the stranger as he disappeared into the inn, making for the semiprivate parlor where she knew all customers of a better sort were accommodated.

Does he think my aunt so unfit to associate with him and his friend, she thought, searching the room for her prey. *Well, I shall make him feel what it means to be so above everyone. I shall treat him,* she vowed, *to an exhibition of vulgarity such as he will never forget.*

A party of ladies and gentlemen sat at nuncheon at one end of the room, and at the other, before the empty hearth, stood the man she sought. Within doors he was even more impressive, his many caped greatcoat just slipping from a pair of broad shoulders clad in an impeccably tailored blue coat, his dark curly head almost brushing the ceiling.

A shaft of sunlight from the window nearby revealed blue eyes beneath arching brows and an arrogant sweep of forehead. His aristocratic nostrils flared and his narrow lips turned down at the corners as he inspected the room with scant approval. He was no older than thirty, Alyssa decided, but his distinct air of experience and fashion made him seem older. Altogether he was an imposing figure, but the memory of his insult to her aunt strengthened her resolve.

"La, sir!," she cried in her best imitation of Aunt Henrietta, advancing on him with a mince and a simper. "What a splendid equipage you have outside, as I made sure of when you was just arriving. Such fine animals, too, that I could not lose a moment in seeking you out to tell you, as I'm sure you'll be gratified to know, that no one in this sad dowdy place has ever seen the like!"

Disregarding his look of revulsion, in which she thought she detected a hint of disappointment, she edged closer and said in a confiding tone, "Of course, we people of fashion all know what is of the first stare, but I'm sure it will do all the poor bumpkins of the neighborhood good just to see such a spectacle."

His brows were now drawn together in a manner that chilled her heart. His eyes, which she now decided were not merely blue, but the color of a sparkling sea, raked her with a contemptuous glance.

Her heart was beating a warning to flee and a blush had risen to her cheeks, but, undaunted, she aimed her last blow. "Why, your clothes, sir, too, are so very much the thing that I fear you will be quite in danger of setting the fashion here!"

His control must be remarkable, she thought with trepidation, because other than his firmly clenched lips, he gave no overt sign of displeasure. With a brief nod and a cold stare that looked right through her, he excused himself.

"You appear to have mistaken me for an acquaintance, madam. If we had ever met, I assure you that I could not help but recall the occasion." And, after one last glance that swept over Alyssa as if evaluating her intentions, origins and the cost of her pelisse all at once, he bowed stiffly and turned away.

His disdain was apparent in every line of his carriage as he left the room, and now Alyssa was all too conscious of the stares and suppressed laughter of the witnesses of the scene.

She mustered as much dignity as she could and followed him out, hoping that she had succeeded in vexing and shaming him more than she had embarrassed herself.

Leaving the inn, she rejoined Henrietta at the linen draper's. "Have you quite finished, Aunt? You know we cannot linger today, as we expect Mr. Noddley at two."

Henrietta, her former unhappiness forgotten in the perusal of silks and muslins, produced her wrapped parcels.

"Oh, I quite remember what day it is, my love. Now here is the lavender muslin, and some more black ribbon, and then some white satin for Clara, though it is too bad she has such a delicate color that white does not become her in the least. She makes a pathetic widow, indeed," she said, sighing. "And today the will is to be read. I am sure I don't know how I will remain composed, seeing Noddley again, poor William's dearest friend!"

A somber mood was now upon her, and Alyssa was occupied in distracting her all the way home, so that she hardly had a moment to reflect on her foolishness in giving a handsome gentleman, obviously of the highest ton, such a disgust of her, all in a fit of pique.

"MADEIRA, SIR?" Phipps, the butler, inquired of the visitor, who stopped pacing long enough to put down the sheaf of papers he had been fanning through his fingers.

Joseph Noddley of Noddley and Webster, Solicitors, eyed the black band around the butler's sleeve, sighed and indicated that some liquid refreshment would not be unwelcome.

He settled himself in a leather-covered desk chair. Poor William's chair, he reminded himself, sipping at the wine and hoping it would imbue him with the courage to face three hysterical females.

Not that Miss Wentworth was ordinarily prone to tears or vapors. No, reflected Noddley as he drained his glass; she was as coolheaded and sensible a young lady as one could hope to meet. But even Miss Alyssa Wentworth, a girl of spirit and good sense, would not be other than shocked to learn that the former trait was to be overridden and the latter subjugated to the mortifying necessity of finding a husband before the year was out.

On Mrs. Clara Wentworth's calm reception of the news, he was not certain he could depend, for it was still too soon after her loss. On Miss Henrietta Wentworth he knew he could not depend at all.

The solicitor rose and went to the sofa at the opposite end of the study. A portrait of his old friend William Wentworth hung above it, and it recalled to him the day he had been summoned to draw up a will. He had faced his friend across the big mahogany desk in that very room, staring at him in disbelief as Mr. Wentworth informed him of his intentions with regard to his estate.

"I know you think it gothic of me to insist on this, Joe, but there it is. I can't leave Finchwood and the fortune to Alyssa unless I can be sure she'll marry. You know the terms of the entail better than I do, I'll warrant. If the direct line fails of male heirs, the heiress must not be a spinster."

Mr. Wentworth had paused to ease his swollen legs onto a footstool. "I know my girl," he continued, "and she's got some independent notions. Daresay it's my own fault for bringing her up to be more educated than her own papa and letting her help me run this place just as if she'd been my son. Be that as it may, Joe," he said, quelling his friend's protest with a look, "she's as good as told me many a time that she has no reason to marry, and no liking for the idea. Not much to wonder at that she wouldn't take kindly to a short rein with all the freedom she's had."

"But surely," Noddley had replied, "she will be able to live quite well on the income you have set aside for her, without also being mistress of Finchwood and the bulk of the fortune. She's a very capable young lady, but why force her to marry against her inclination? Would not the next heir, your great-nephew, do as well?"

"What!" The sudden purple flush of Mr. Wentworth's face had alarmed his friend. "Leave my beautiful Finchwood and my hard-earned money to that slithering macaroni, that jumped-up coxcomb?" William Wentworth pounded on the desktop. "Never! He's no better than his father and grandfather before him. Can't understand what possessed my Aunt Amelia to marry the fellow, and at her age, too. Her grandson, Henry Basking, is a cursed loose fish, and would sell this place and everything in it to pay his debts and add to his snuffbox collection. No, my girl must marry. It would be a disaster for the estate to fall into Basking's hands. And while she's at it, it ought to be a titled gentleman, because she's got her mother's blood as well as mine, and she's a right to all that goes with it."

The solicitor knew when to concede defeat, and at length the will was drawn up, signed and witnessed.

Noddley came back to the present abruptly as the door to the study opened and Alyssa Wentworth entered.

"My dear…" He went to greet her and clasped both of her small hands in his.

"Dear Mr. Noddley, it is so good to see you again," she said in her warm, melodious voice, returning the pressure of his hands. Petite, but elegantly formed, with her burnt-gold hair and large, lustrous green eyes, his old friend's child was undeniably a beautiful young woman. Too beautiful, he thought, to be hidden away here. Perhaps, then, it would all be for the best. But would the ton see anything but a tradesman's daughter?

"How are you ladies managing?" he asked in a fatherly tone, noting the unusual droop to her full lips and the paleness of her cheeks.

She managed a smile. "We're getting on very well, considering. Clara is bearing up splendidly, although she is still a trifle overset. To lose two husbands before one is two and thirty simply does not bear thinking of! As for me—" Her smile faded and her lower lip trembled for a moment. "Of course I miss Papa dreadfully. We became closer than ever after he sold the company. And he was feeling much better, so it was a great shock when he—'' She could not continue.

Mr. Noddley swallowed past a lump in his throat. He and William Wentworth had been friends since boyhood. He cursed the business on the continent that had kept him from the deathbed.

Alyssa had recovered. ''My aunt Henrietta is still sadly cast down. Clara and I have been trying so hard to bring up her spirits that we scarcely have time to brood.''

''I am sorry that Miss Wentworth is not up to hearing the will read.'' Secretly relieved, for the Madeira had not added an ounce to his courage, Noddley looked forward to having one less case of hysteria to deal with.

''Oh, Aunt Henrietta will be down at any moment,'' replied Alyssa, blithely disabusing him of this comforting notion. She smiled again. ''She is not too sunk in grief to lose all curiosity about her brother's will. My aunt is the dearest creature, but so entirely predictable.''

The door opened to admit Mrs. Clara Wentworth. Alyssa's stepmother was a fair, youthful-looking woman of middling height, with graceful carriage and a sweet expression.

''Mr. Noddley! I am very happy to see you again after all these months.''

''Indeed, ma'am,'' said the solicitor, taking the hand she offered. ''That business on the continent was most vexatious, when with all my heart I longed to be here. I had left instructions with my staff that no one but myself was to handle this matter, since it is rather confidential.''

These words provoked a glance of curiosity from Alyssa, and he wished again that his friend had consented to inform the girl earlier. Now it was too late to spare her the shock.

"It is of no importance," Clara assured him. "Eight months ago we could not have sat through it. We were content to wait for your return.''

She had begun to inquire about the health of Mr. Noddley's family, when their attention was suddenly drawn to the doorway, where a most spectacularly attired female was making a dramatic entrance.

Miss Henrietta Wentworth was dressed in such extravagant mourning that she outshone even the widow. Her gown of black silk was trimmed with such an abundance of braid, ruffles, frogging and lace that she resembled a life-size dressmaker's doll displaying various types of ornamentation.

Her sleeves were hugely puffed at the shoulder and buttoned tightly down her plump arms with big jet buttons. A black hat with a nodding plume sat above her frizzled brown fringe of hair, and a small red nose and double chin peeped out from beneath a gauzy black veil.

In one of her plump hands she carried a vast handkerchief, lavishly trimmed with lace, and in the other a beaded reticule, which Noddley suspected of containing a reviving vinaigrette.

This apparition, when it noticed Mr. Noddley, rushed forward with an awful cry of grief and threw itself upon the unwary solicitor, enfolding him in a crushing embrace.

"Oh, dear Joseph! He is gone, my dearest brother, your old friend! Oh, what is to become of us?" sobbed Miss Wentworth.

Noddley, his worst fears confirmed, turned crimson and vainly tried to stem the flow of her tears while struggling to free himself from her grasp.

"Now, Miss Wentworth, please do not distress yourself . . . Henrietta, do try to remain composed."

Clara and Alyssa, after exchanging looks of mingled amusement and exasperation, went to his rescue and led the lady firmly to a sofa. Noddley, relieved of his burden, straightened his crumpled neckcloth and poured a glass of Madeira for the sufferer. She accepted it with a look of tearful gratitude and proceeded to down the entire glass in a gulp, much to Noddley's amazement, for he had never seen a lady do more than sip at a glass of wine.

Mindful of the likely effect of the contents of the will on such delicate sensibilities, he took Alyssa aside.

"Miss Henrietta is still in such great distress that I fear she will only become more agitated as we proceed. Perhaps you can persuade her to retire until we have done."

The wine had not dulled any of that lady's senses, for Henrietta immediately raised her head and cried, "What? Did you say I may not stay and hear my dear brother's will? No, I must be strong—I will be strong! Dear William, I am sure, would have wanted me to be present." With this she planted herself more firmly on the sofa, lest anyone should dare try removing her.

Noddley resigned himself to the inevitable scene. "Very well. I suggest we begin."

CHAPTER TWO

NODDLEY MOVED behind the desk and picked up his papers, clearing his throat and avoiding Alyssa's eye.

The ladies took seats opposite, Clara quiet and composed, Alyssa calm and keeping a watchful eye on her aunt, who snuffled into her handkerchief, over which she steadily regarded Mr. Noddley. The solicitor had read nearly two paragraphs of the document, concerned with some minor bequests, when the sounds of a disturbance came to their ears. A moment later the door to the study was flung open by a stranger, a much agitated Phipps directly on his heels.

"What is the meaning of this intrusion?" bellowed Mr. Noddley, very much startled by the sudden entrance of a scrawny young man, every inch of whose attire proclaimed him to be one of the dandy set.

"I beg your pardon, Mrs. Wentworth, but this person..." Phipps said with an indignant look at the diminutive stranger, "demanded to see you at once, and when I told him that on no account were you to be disturbed, he—"

"I said that I would show myself in. I am, after all, one of the family, and this is undoubtedly a family occasion," drawled the visitor, sweeping the room with a derisive glance.

For a moment everyone simply stared. Henrietta was bowled over with admiration for the gentleman's dress, which consisted of a coat of green-and-white striped Bath cloth, under which reposed not one, but two waistcoats, one plain and one striped. Above these rested an enormous starched cravat, arranged in intricate folds and ornamented by a large jeweled pin.

The points of his collar reached past his sharp chin and threatened to engulf his ears, huge though they were. Pantaloons of a delicate shade of primrose drew the eye down to a pair of gleaming, tasseled Hessians. Fobs and seals galore hung from this personage, and no less than four rings adorned his well-tended hands, in which he held a gold-topped walking stick and a high-crowned beaver hat. In short, none of the ladies had ever seen anything quite like the picture he presented.

Alyssa stared quite as hard as the others, not merely in amazement, but trying her best to call to mind his identity, for she was sure they had met at least once before. His narrow gray eyes, mere slits in a catlike face, and his thinning hair of an undecided brownish hue nagged at her memory. Finally her cogitation produced the desired result.

Surprising her companions and, she was sure, utterly spoiling the effect the visitor had hoped to produce, she calmly welcomed him.

"Of course, how silly of me to forget. You are my cousin, Henry Basking. How do you do?"

Mr. Basking recovered quickly and made the ladies an elegant leg. "Well done, coz. I was not certain that you would recall our last meeting, as we were both mere children at the time." He giggled like a child as

he said it, though surely, Alyssa thought, he was close
to thirty. "However, I am sure you will not dispute my
right to remain, for if I am correct, this worthy fellow
is about to inform you of the manner in which Great-
Uncle William's property is to be disposed of."

Noddley bristled at this impudence. "You happen
to be correct, sir. However, as to your right to be
here—"

Alyssa, who wondered how her cousin had known
about the will being read that day, could not imagine
why he wished to hear it. "It's all right, Mr. Noddley.
Perhaps Mr. Basking has an expectation of a bequest.
By all means, let us continue."

Basking glanced around the room, Alyssa thought,
much like one who sought an estimate of the value of
the furnishings.

"You are right, cousin. When I inherit my grandfather's title I will come into very little in the way of
fortune. My mother and I live on a rather limited income," he said with a casual glance down at his elaborate costume, "and so I must see to it that we receive
any inheritance due us from the other side of the family. My grandmother was, after all, a Wentworth," he
concluded, thrusting his hat and stick at a seething
Phipps, who carried them away in disgust.

"Nonsense," mumbled Mr. Noddley, and gave the
intruder a scathing glance. "Mrs. Wentworth, I really
do not—"

"Pray continue reading, Mr. Noddley," said
Alyssa, prepared to suffer her cousin's presence rather
than prolong the proceedings by argument.

"Indeed," said Clara, "there is no reason why Mr.
Basking cannot hear the will."

"Oh, dear me, none at all," Henrietta chimed in.

Mr. Noddley sighed and resigned himself to the inevitable, while a smug expression settled on Mr. Basking's countenance.

Mr. Wentworth had provided handsomely for his wife and sister from the income and property he had accumulated during his lifetime. But the bulk of his fortune, including the house and extensive holdings at Finchwood, derived from the estate bequested by his father, with its restrictive entail. It was as he prepared to read the paragraphs pertaining to this that Mr. Noddley looked up anxiously, clearing his throat.

Alyssa could not help but notice the nervousness of the solicitor and the eagerness of Basking at that moment. She could not imagine the cause of either. Surely, she thought, her papa could not at the last moment have decided she was unfit to manage the estate, when for the past few years he had prepared her for that very role. Her own name jogged her out of her musings.

"To my daughter Alyssa, I leave the estate of Finchwood, my shares in the Buttingdon cotton mill, my interest in the Cloverly shipping company and all other income not heretofore bequeathed. However, in compliance with the entail under which this estate was placed by my father, George Wentworth, she may not take possession of it if she is still unmarried within a year of the date this will is made known. She is to marry a gentleman of rank, titled and of suitable social position. In default of these conditions being met, the estate will pass to the next heir, Henry Basking, grandson of my aunt, Amelia Wentworth Basking."

Fearfully Mr. Noddley looked up from his papers, and saw that Alyssa's face had gone white. Clara's countenance registered sheer disbelief, and Henrietta's mouth had fallen completely open, causing her chins to droop over her black lace collar in a most unfortunate manner. The solicitor was relieved to observe, however, that not a single fit of vapors appeared to be imminent.

Henry Basking, looking extremely pleased with himself, was the first to speak. "I see that my late relative has provided you with a little surprise. Although I did not know him well, I must say that I am not as shocked as everyone else seems to be."

He looked at Alyssa with a half leer, half pitying smile. "It seems that Great-Uncle William kept the fact of the entail from his dear daughter, although it intimately affects her chance of inheriting. Pardon my boldness, fair cousin, but perhaps he knew how unlikely it would be for you to make such a match, and did not care to see you embarrass yourself in the attempt while he was alive. For what man of good family would marry the daughter of a man whose own father began as a common weaver?"

Alyssa rose and clenched her hands to keep them from shaking. She turned to her cousin, her eyes darkening with rage.

"How dare you, sir! You have forced your way into our home and still have been treated with more courtesy than you deserve. Now you attempt to insult me and my family. As you were so perceptive as to guess, I had not been informed of the condition attached to my inheritance, but whatever my father's reason for it—" her voice faltered momentarily "—I am sure it was a good one, and I have confidence that I will be able to fulfill the requirement within the year. And in the process I shall take the utmost delight in depriving a creature like yourself of every penny of that fortune."

She moved swiftly and rang for Phipps. "Your behavior has been intolerable. Please remove yourself from our home and do not return."

"Perhaps, coz, I shall return when it is *my* home," he said, and before she could escape he was upon her and taking her hand in his. He would have pressed it to his lips if she had not torn it away. He chuckled.

"Or perhaps, one day, *our* home?"

"You make yourself ridiculous," said Alyssa icily, turning away.

"Do I?" he inquired, not in the least insulted. "You must admit that your background, despite your mother's good birth, will give you no entrée into the privileged circles of the beau monde. This will make your task difficult, if not impossible. On the other hand, we Baskings, although impecunious, are a family with impeccable credentials. Why even Grandmother Wentworth, from such a humble background, was received with the deference due the wife of a Basking. You may wish to keep in mind, sweet coz, that on grandfather's demise I will assume the title, and the expectation of that qualifies me to join with you in defeating this wretched entail."

Alyssa was thoroughly revolted by his oily, insinuating manner, and was intensely relieved when Phipps appeared, accompanied by a giant of a footman, who stood menacingly by the door.

With a wary glance at this forbidding individual and another deep bow to the ladies, Mr. Basking finally departed.

The room was silent for a moment, as if they all drew breath at once, and then Henrietta cried, "Oh, that horrid little man! I cannot like him. Though, to be sure, his clothes are very fine."

"I am so sorry, my love," said Clara in a solemn tone. She looked as confused as Alyssa felt. "Your papa never told me about this entail, and if he had mentioned it I would have urged him to apprise you of it at once. I would not have believed that William could be so unfeeling as to keep it from you."

"Indeed," Mr. Noddley hastened to explain, "I urged him to explain it to the child, but he had the idea that—" he turned to Alyssa, slightly embarrassed. "Well, let us say that you were in no great hurry to wed, that you valued your independence, and so he was loath to force you to it before it was necessary."

"Well, she is forced to do it now," said Henrietta irritably, taking to her handkerchief once more. "And she has only one year!"

Alyssa tried to dissolve the tension and attempted a smile. "I am surprised, but I cannot be resentful when I recall that this is exactly Papa's way. Besides, wouldn't you rather see me married, even if by necessity, than to see Finchwood fall into Henry Basking's hands?"

Mr. Noddley coughed. "I am glad, my dear, that you are taking it so well. But I must explain that although your grandfather did not wish the estate to be managed by a spinster, it was your papa who decided your husband should be a peer. Although if this

Basking fellow is any example, I should say you'd be better off with an honest tradesman!''

Now Alyssa's smile came more naturally. "It is not so shocking, Mr. Noddley. We all know how Papa felt about being shunned by society simply because he had earned his fortune. It especially hurt him on poor Mama's account. She gave up a whole way of life for him and suffered from her family's rejection. I completely understand his making the extra condition. Besides, if I am to do this thing, why do it by halves? I daresay it is just as easy to fall in love with a peer as with an ordinary fellow.''

The solicitor laughed, and even Henrietta had to smile.

"No doubt, my dear," said Noddley, "yet I don't believe you should be thinking in terms of a—hmm, romantic attachment. There will hardly be time for that. No, you will simply have to do your best to gain acceptance into the proper circles. Perhaps your mother's family, if they are willing to acknowledge you, can help. Then you must hope for an eligible man to make you an offer. A fellow would have to be blind and stupid not to!'' His irritation at the ways of the world overcame him. "But, no, I'm afraid that falling in love is a luxury you cannot afford.''

"Well, I shan't think of that until I know that Finchwood is safe from Henry Basking. My papa was as fine a man, or finer, than any debt-ridden peer or petty landowner with only his name to recommend him. I am quite resigned to carrying out his wishes, so we had best see about procuring an introduction to the ton, otherwise not a single title will come my way.''

"Lord, it is so brave of you!" said Henrietta. "You have only a year, and how can you hope to go into society when we know no one of consequence in town? I don't consider, of course, poor William's business associates, for I am sure they are nobody at all."

"Henrietta, dear—" Clara began.

"And then there is the difficulty about the mourning," continued Henrietta. "It's not proper for us to go about in society so soon . . . that is, if we are to attend you as your chaperones," she added hopefully.

Alyssa smiled at her aunt's expression, for she knew that Henrietta had long cherished an ambition to live the life of lady of fashion in town. "I should be desolate without my loved ones to support me in such a situation," she assured her, "and as to the mourning, why, I'm sure Papa would have preferred us to put off our black before a year is out than to have Henry Basking inherit Finchwood."

Clara could not hide her anxiety. "We shall try our best, of course," she said, twisting a scrap of handkerchief, "but what can we do if no one in the ton wishes to form a connection with you because of the old scandal of your parents' elopement? How will you avoid falling prey to a mere fortune hunter?"

Mr. Noddley ventured an opinion. "I must say I agree with Mrs. Wentworth. You will need an introduction to the right people, and then you must hope that a suitable gentleman will, er—"

Here Alyssa interrupted him, for a daring idea had taken root in her mind. With it came a hope that her task might not be as impossible as it seemed.

"I will not sit waiting with folded hands for a gentleman to come and make me an offer," she announced, and walked briskly to the door. "Mr. Noddley, I'm going to need your assistance. Please join me in the sitting room in a quarter of an hour. Clara and Aunt Henrietta, I shall see you at tea." Noting their furrowed brows, she added, "And please do not worry so. It is all very simple. You'll see." She left the room with a firm, determined stride, her eyes faraway.

"Whatever does the child mean?" wondered Henrietta aloud.

Clara was equally bewildered, but said to the solicitor, "We can be sure of one thing—she will find a way to do it. Alyssa loves Finchwood too much to lose it, even if it means giving up her independence. I only hope she will not be obliged to marry someone unsuitable, for she could not be happy as the wife of a man she could not respect, or who would not respect her." She shook her head. "I fear it will end badly."

"Come, now, my dear Mrs. Wentworth, this is not like your usual optimism. Remember whose daughter she is. She is as proud and stubborn as William himself." He patted her hand reassuringly. "I don't know what she means to do, but since she had the sense to ask for my help, I'll see to it that she comes to no harm. You can depend upon it."

CHAPTER THREE

THE SOLICITOR FOUND Miss Wentworth in the sitting room, at a small escritoire situated to get the full benefit of the garden view. She was applying a wafer to a missive she had just finished writing, and began another note without looking up as he entered.

"Come in, sir. I'm sending a note to the housekeeper in Green Street so that she may have the house ready for us in a fortnight's time. We leave the Tuesday after next."

Noddley was made uneasy by this abrupt decision, but she ignored his harrumphing, finished the second note and sealed it.

"There! This is to my old school friend, Mary Carstairs. She married a young man of good family, and from what she writes, I would say that they are not exactly shunned by the ton. And yet, Mary's father was not of very elevated birth himself."

She tilted her head and smiled at Noddley. "Perhaps people are not such high sticklers now as they were when my parents married."

"Then you should not have a great deal of trouble fulfilling the conditions of your father's will," said the solicitor, observing these preparations with increasing dismay. "But I beg, my dear, that you do nothing, er, hasty. It would not do to . . . that is . . ."

Alyssa kindly put him out of his misery. "Why, poor Mr. Noddley! Have I frightened you by saying I *would not wait* for an offer to be made to me? Perhaps you feared I would place an advertisement in the *Morning Post*, to whit, 'Well-looking young female, considerable heiress, seeks agreeable gentleman to provide title in return for comfortable estate and regular income.'"

Mr. Noddley laughed uncertainly. "Come, now, miss, enough teasing. Tell this poor old man just exactly what you are plotting."

The mischief flickered out of Alyssa's green eyes and she was repentant. "I'm sorry, dear sir. Please sit down." She indicated a delicate chair beside her desk. "I shall tell you—only please don't object until you have heard all I have to say."

"I am sure you will agree," Alyssa began, "that since my circumstances are so unusual and my time so limited, the usual manner of finding a husband will provide me with no surety that by the end of the year I will have one. So I have decided that I will take a more active role than merely inserting myself into the ton and awaiting the gentleman's attentions."

Mr. Noddley swallowed and said faintly, "A—a more active role?"

"Yes," she replied firmly. "I am going to learn as much as I can about the ton. I want to know all about the people who rule society, and about where I should be seen, where I should never appear. I want you to compile a report for me—"

"My dear Miss Wentworth!" Noddley stood and stared in amazement.

"My dear Mr. Noddley! I am going about this in the only sensible way, surely you can see that. This is much too important a matter to leave to chance. And that is not all. You must find out for me the names of several gentlemen who might make an appropriate...whom I might...well, since I am forced to marry, I would like to choose the man myself." In spite of her bravado, she could not meet the solicitor's gaze and stared instead at the shrubs outside her window. "From a list which you will draw up."

"Your papa would have had my head for such a thing!" exploded Noddley, beginning to pace the room in his agitation.

"I am sorry, sir, if this displeases you, but I cannot afford to sit waiting for some snobbish fool whose need for money will overcome his distaste for my origins to ask for my hand. I don't believe I will be welcomed into the fashionable world without a great effort on my part to put myself forward. I need your help. Please, please say I can rely on you. After all, you are in a position to discover what I need to know, and did you not say that I must be able to protect myself from fortune hunters? At least this way we will know that the gentlemen in question are suitable."

After his first shock began to subside, Noddley had to admit that however distasteful her plan, the girl showed remarkable coolheadedness in the face of what should have been a severe blow.

"And just how, Miss Wentworth," he asked, relenting a bit, "after I provide you with this list of *suitable* gentlemen, are you going to induce the one you select to make you an offer? Or will you turn the tables entirely and make the offer yourself?"

"Leave the rest to me," she said airily, but in truth she shrank from that extremity. There was plenty of time to think about it, she told herself, once she had chosen the man. "This is my only hope. All I ask is that you provide the facts I need. I am depending on you, Mr. Noddley. I—I have no one else to turn to now."

The solicitor was won over in the end. He could not shirk his responsibility to his friend's daughter now. The least he could do, he thought, was see to it that she knew enough about the world she was trying to enter to protect herself from its less scrupulous denizens.

"I will do my best to help you, child, and we can only hope that your cousin Basking does not try to stir up the old scandal about your Mama and Papa's elopement. If the gossips begin talking . . . suppose he puts it about that you were on the catch for a titled husband?"

"As to that," Alyssa replied, "it is hardly likely that I would be the first woman ever to come to town with that purpose in mind. Besides, there must be some members of my mother's family left, and perhaps I can persuade them to champion me. You must try to find out."

"Very well." The solicitor sighed heavily. "I'll return to London tomorrow morning and begin these . . . investigations—" he shuddered "—right away."

"And please—" Alyssa put a hand on his sleeve "—not a word of any of this to Clara or Aunt Henrietta. I don't want them to know anything except that you are finding out how we should proceed once in town."

Mr. Noddley promised to keep the plan secret, and they went to join the ladies for tea.

To Alyssa's relief, neither her stepmother nor her aunt plagued her with questions about her plans, though Clara looked at her with concern and Henrietta was bubbling over with suppressed curiosity.

Watching as her plump aunt made a hearty meal of bread and cakes, she reflected that neither of her prospective chaperons was entirely suitable for the role.

Henrietta was childishly simple sometimes, and her manners were too informal and unrestrained to be pleasing to the fashionable world. Clara was extremely sensible, but so youthful-looking that no one would think her a suitable chaperon, either. Besides, without feeling any disloyalty to her father's memory, Alyssa intended that her stepmother should have the opportunity to meet some gentlemen and perhaps remarry. Her chances would be nil if she had to sit against the wall at every gathering, chatting with the dowagers, while keeping an eye on Alyssa.

"Well, my love," Clara's soft voice interrupted her stepdaughter's reflections, "have you and Mr. Noddley decided on something?"

"Oh, yes, we have conjured up a plan between us," Alyssa replied, smiling reassuringly at the nervous solicitor. "I have written to Mrs. Oliver to prepare the house in Green Street for us. If you have no objection, I should like to leave in a fortnight."

"So soon," Clara murmured, smoothing the folds of her black skirt.

Alyssa went to her and took her hand. "I know exactly what you must feel. It is not a year since Papa left us, and it would be unnatural for you to be in spirits for going about the town. But it is a sacrifice we all must make, for it is Papa who is asking us to make it.''

Clara sighed and assured her that she was prepared to make any sacrifice to help her obey her father's last wishes.

Henrietta, too, was momentarily surprised by the suddenness with which their new life was to begin, but soon grew accustomed to the idea of abandoning her role as a mourner and taking on one as a member of the ton. ''Well, if it is all decided, then I must look to my wardrobe. Heaven knows, I cannot travel in the old green kerseymere!'' And with that she excused herself to survey her gowns.

While Mr. Noddley visited the estate office to confer with the manager, Alyssa took advantage of Clara's assurance that she would not mind being left alone with a book to take a late-afternoon ride.

After putting on her gray habit trimmed with black braid, a matching high-crowned, veiled hat and her boots, she picked up her crop and gloves and headed for the stables. Her mare was soon made ready and a groom handed her into the saddle, mounted his own horse and followed her at a discreet distance.

At length she urged the mare into a trot and felt her worries fade as her pleasure in the exercise and the sunny day soothed her troubled spirits. Ten minutes of brisk riding brought her to the border of the property, and after walking her horse for some minutes, she stopped in front of the hedge, which formed a boundary. Absently she gazed at the adjoining estate, while her thoughts turned inexorably back to her dilemma.

She could not accept the idea of failure, or the thought of Finchwood going to Henry Basking. If it came to that, she might have to marry him, if she could still retain some control so that he might not ruin the estate with his spendthrift ways. The thought made her shudder, but she assured herself it would be a marriage of convenience only.

But perhaps she was too pessimistic. He could not be that formidable an enemy. In spite of his vaunted impeccable social position, she was sure he would not be considered a desirable match by the mothers of eligible girls.

Yes, the daughter of a wealthy cit was probably all that Basking could hope for, and Alyssa knew, without shame, that that was exactly what she was. But despite her pride in her father, she had always identified a great deal with the world of fashion and bon ton that her mother had given up to marry William Wentworth.

There had been some talk of giving Alyssa a season in London, but Mr. Wentworth had not been in favor of the idea, and Mrs. Wentworth, shunned by society, was not at all sure they could pull it off. Alyssa had spent some time at a fashionable young ladies' academy in Bath, where she learned as much or more of French, Italian, dancing and needlework as any young lady of the most noble birth could boast. But when she returned home after her mother's untimely death, there was no more talk of London. In between school terms, she and her father grew very close, and Alyssa forgot any girlish social ambition she might have had in the thrill of being mistress in all but name of Finchwood.

She recalled now with a smile how furious she had been when, at seventeen, after her last term in Bath, she had come home to find that her father intended to remarry. How soon her anger had evaporated after meeting Clara, sweet tempered and scarcely a dozen years older than her, seeming more like a sister than a stepmother.

At home with her father and Clara, Alyssa had been too content to worry about her future, and though she had some beaux in the neighborhood, she took none of them seriously. William, as his health declined, had admitted that he wanted to keep his little girl with him a while longer, and Clara was too fond of her to insist on vigorous husband hunting for her stepdaughter. Then, too, her father had been well aware that Alyssa had no eagerness to submit herself to any authority but his own.

And now I must have a husband, Alyssa thought, parting with her memories under the heavy necessity of the present. She knew that even if luck were with her, whatever husband she chose would wish to be master. Even her dear indulgent papa had expected to rule supreme. But not to marry would be to lose everything dear to her, and to see her home, heritage and fortune go to a man who was not fit to polish her father's boots.

Yet the thought of the reception that undoubtedly awaited her in London chilled her. She recalled the superior air of the man she had impulsively insulted in the village earlier that day. Most people of fashion would no doubt be very like him, and would react in much the same manner when faced with the daughter of a tradesman.

Her sense of humor suddenly bubbled through the layers of worry and she smiled, thinking how foolish that elegant gentleman of the bang-up curricle would feel if he happened to meet her at some exclusive event. But she vowed to keep her temper no matter how unkindly she was received and to put a strict guard on her manners and behavior.

As if through a dense fog, the sound of hoofbeats penetrated her consciousness. Alyssa had to turn her attention to controlling the mare, whose ears flicked forward as she danced nervously.

From the woods of the adjoining lands emerged two figures on horseback, the first one slowing when he caught sight of Alyssa and calling to his companion, who wheeled his horse. Alyssa was conscious of an increasing horror as the two gentlemen approached the hedge.

One was unknown to her, a slim blond man of some five and thirty years of age, with a weathered complexion and a small white scar at the corner of his mouth. His riding clothes were tailored in a military cut, and he controlled his chestnut gelding with ease. It was the other gentleman whose appearance had caused the breath to depart from Alyssa's lungs and her heart to leap to her throat, for he was none other than the haughty stranger of the village inn.

For a moment they stared at each other, he with an expression of distaste and she with a countenance registering sheer panic. In the absence of an intent to avenge an insult, Alyssa felt no desire to continue her ridiculous masquerade. Besides, the other gentleman was already greeting her and she was too bemused to do other than reply in a normal, polite fashion.

"You must be one of my neighbors, from Finch-wood, perhaps?" said the blond man. "My name's Talbot, Sir Edward Talbot. I'm the new owner of Oakhill."

Alyssa forced her eyes away from the steely gaze of the other man and extended a friendly hand to Sir Edward. With only a fleeting thought of just how her acquaintance of the morning was going to accept her true identity, she introduced herself. "You are correct, sir. Finchwood is my home, and as a neighbor I'm very pleased to know that Oakhill has a new master."

He shook her hand warmly. "If all my new neighbors are as welcoming, I'm sure I shall be happy here." He turned to glance at his companion, who was lagging some distance behind. "Come, Brookmere, and meet my charming neighbor, Miss Wentworth—"

He broke off and turned back to Alyssa. "I fell in love with the old place." He gestured toward the Tudor manor in the distance. "But the previous owner was neglectful and I've a great deal of work ahead of me. My friend, the Viscount Charles Brookmere, has consented to advise me. I quite rely on him. Ah, here you are! Never knew you to be so slow to greet a lady before."

He performed the introduction with a flourish, in the attitude of one who is presenting a rare treat to a friend, and Alyssa held her breath. She was uncertain of what to expect from him and was relieved when he simply bowed over her hand and politely expressed his pleasure in the introduction. But there was a clouded expression in his blue eyes and she could tell his mind was working furiously, trying to decide if she was indeed the vulgar person who had accosted him that morning.

Noting the automatic difference in his manner when presented to a presumably ladylike female, she decided to conquer her fear of his reaction and disabuse him of any doubt on this point.

"Welcome to our neighborhood, my lord." She gave him her sweetest smile, but her eyes held a challenge. "I hope you are pleased with it. I think you need have no fear for your friend's comfort, for he has picked a charming country home, has he not? Oakhill is situated near one of the most pleasant villages in Kent."

She had expected to discomfit him, and was thrown off by his immediate assumption of complaisance. "Indeed," he replied, "I find that my opinion of it has risen considerably since this morning. But that, I hope, may be attributed to the fact that I suffered an accident to my curricle, which delayed my arrival at Oakhill. I am afraid I was not half so pleased with my friend's new situation *then*, as I am now."

Challenge accepted and battle offered, he gazed at her expectantly.

Sir Edward was looking at the two of them as if they had quite lost their minds. "Well! You are an odd fish today, Brookmere. Never known you to be so talkative at first meeting before, either."

Alyssa felt her face grow warm. She had quite forgotten the presence of her friendly new neighbor. But he good-naturedly ignored her mysterious embarrassment, and went on to question her about the neighborhood and its inhabitants, until she was conversing quite naturally. Brookmere looked on silently, but did not take his eyes from her face. Once or twice she glanced at him, but only in the set of his lips did she see any hint of amusement or irritation at the way she had tricked him.

The clouds began to cover what remained of the sun, and Alyssa excused herself, as it was almost time to dress for dinner. With luck, she thought, she would not have to meet with Lord Brookmere again. But she could not refuse when the sociable Sir Edward begged to be allowed to wait upon her one morning and meet her family.

"My aunt and stepmother would be delighted to receive you," she assured him. At least, she thought, here was one person of apparent consequence who could not tell that the Wentworths were not fit to associate with.

"And I, Miss Wentworth?" Lord Brookmere's deep tones startled her. "Will I also be made welcome at Finchwood?" Now he was smiling, but it was a deliberate and provoking smile.

She swallowed and tried to look nonchalant. "Of course, my lord." Then, returning his smile with real enjoyment, she added, "And my aunt will be ecstatic to receive a visit from such a fine gentleman. You and she will rub along together famously, I trust!" With a wave at Sir Edward, she turned her horse and headed for home.

CHAPTER FOUR

HENRIETTA WAS GULPING DOWN her chocolate and swallowing many dainty morsels of toast when Alyssa entered the breakfast parlor next morning.

"You are early today, Aunt," she remarked as she sat down and a footman poured her coffee.

Henrietta, replete at last, pushed back from the table. "I was much too excited to stay abed! There is so much to do to prepare for our journey!"

Alyssa smiled as she buttered her toast, knowing very well that all the responsibility of the arrangements would fall on her, Clara and the servants. Henrietta could not even be counted on to supervise the packing of her own gowns without driving her maid to distraction.

Henrietta stood up and fluttered to the door, dropping a kiss on her niece's cheek on her way. "I must see the dressmaker today. But I shall not be gone long, and if the gentlemen you met yesterday should happen to call, you will contrive, won't you, to keep them here until I return? I would so like to meet them!"

Alyssa promised to do her best, but secretly she hoped that Sir Edward would be too busy at Oakhill to perform his promised visit so soon. She had not felt brave enough to reveal to her aunt the identity of Sir

Edward's companion, imagining Henrietta's raptures and Lord Brookmere's probable response.

The entrance of Mr. Noddley, heavy eyed and all but silent, removed this worry temporarily from her mind. She watched as Henrietta greeted the solicitor with an effusiveness almost equal to that of the day before.

A night's fitful sleep had done nothing to relieve the solicitor's anxiety about his young client's predicament, but he could think of no way to dissuade her. "If you don't mind, my dear, I should like to leave for town right after breakfast. I believe you will agree that the sooner I begin my inves—" He stopped, aware that Henrietta still lingered and was listening eagerly. "That is, our arrangements, the easier it will be for you ladies." Alyssa made no objection, and disappointed that no further nuggets were forthcoming, Henrietta went on her way.

Clara entered, with shadowed eyes that told the tale of a night similar to Mr. Noddley's. Her sentiments were in complete agreement with the solicitor's, though she knew not even half as much as he did of her stepdaughter's intentions.

Alyssa covered the breakfast hour with inconsequential chatter of London, clothes and their new neighbor, in an attempt to distract Clara from wondering about her plans. She was glad of Noddley's presence, for she did not wish to be left to the mercy of her stepmother's gentle but persistent inquiries.

The solicitor finished one last cup of coffee, rose and began to take his leave of them. "I shall be in correspondence with you, Miss Wentworth, regarding the, er...arrangements." He shot a meaningful glance at Alyssa, and she was hard put not to laugh at his serious manner. Although her task was a difficult one, nothing about it, she vowed, would make her sink into gloom.

When Mr. Noddley had gone, Alyssa invented some very plausible tasks that would take her out of Clara's presence. Thus it was not until the morning was far advanced that the ladies were together again, and neither Clara nor Henrietta had any opportunity to question Alyssa, for she fled to her room to make a hasty repair to her toilette, with some thoughts of escaping again for a ride before dinner. In this, however, she was to be thwarted for just as she emerged from her chamber, a young housemaid breathlessly accosted her.

"Oh, miss, please, miss, Mr. Phipps says as how I'm to tell you that two gentlemen have called, and that Mrs. Wentworth and Miss Henrietta is receiving them in the drawing room, if you please."

Alyssa thanked her and descended the stairs, her pulse tumultuous. She had not really expected the visit so soon, and the thought of Henrietta exposed to the scathing glances of Lord Brookmere made her quake. It was only to be hoped that he would remember his manners in front of his friend, at least.

When she reached the drawing room, all seemed cordial. Clara and Henrietta were entertaining their guests without the slightest sign of strain on anyone's part. The two gentlemen, seated on striped satin chairs, held glasses of wine and were sharing a plate of ratafia biscuits. Sir Edward was conversing animatedly with Clara, and Lord Brookmere, to Alyssa's amazement, was the calm recipient of Henrietta's version of the Wentworth family history.

"Ah, Miss Wentworth!" Sir Edward rose eagerly at her entrance. "I have been telling Mrs. Wentworth how much I admire the style of your home. Your grandpapa who built it must have been a man of excellent taste, wouldn't you say, Brookmere?" He turned an innocent and enthusiastic face to his friend, who, to Alyssa's satisfaction, finally looked the slightest bit discomfited.

"A most ingenious gentleman, to be sure," he said, not meeting Alyssa's gaze.

"Oh, yes, and my brother, William, so like him!" cried Henrietta. "A natural gentleman, and such a head for business!"

Barely pausing for breath, she turned to Sir Edward. "Do you make a long stay in the country, sir? I fear, in any case, that we will not enjoy your company for long, for we go to town in a fortnight," she said with an air of importance.

Sir Edward assured her that he regretted their intended departure. Although his companion's face was a closed book, he, at least, seemed to find Miss Wentworth's manners amusing.

"But never fear, I shan't be too dull here. Brookmere has promised to advise me on the matter of setting Oakhill to rights, and we shall be engaged from sunup till sundown. So kind of him, too, to let me drag him away from all his town engagements. He is in great demand by all the best hostesses, I assure you," he said, and flashed a crooked grin.

Alyssa could well believe this, for the viscount's air and bearing were as fashionable as anyone could wish.

Indeed she was surprised that he was content to rusticate when the temptations of London called to him.

"My friend is too prejudiced in my favor, I fear," said Lord Brookmere with an unexpected smile. However snobbish his ideas, thought Alyssa, he had a real fondness for Sir Edward. "After many seasons, the enjoyments of town begin to lose their allure."

Henrietta, vastly impressed by both the visitors, could not refrain from begging them for details of the London fashions and the latest *on-dit*.

"Do tell me, what is the latest news? We live sadly retired here, and I vow I haven't been to town in a twelvemonth!" Without allowing time for a reply, she went on, "Is it true what they say of long sleeves? And that it is no longer the mode to dampen one's petticoat to wear under muslin?"

Clara started at this, and would have gently reproved her, but Henrietta, leaning forward so that her flesh strained against her stays, whispered dramatically, "And is it true what they say of the Princess Caroline? Such shocking stories!"

Alyssa cast a desperate glance at the viscount, who showed neither surprise nor disgust, but sat like a man of stone, determined not to be provoked and to reveal nothing.

"Henrietta, dear," said Clara, placing a restraining hand on her sister-in-law's arm, "you know that we had letters from the Misses Fuller in town not a week ago, and that gentlemen are not interested in fashion and gossip."

"To the contrary, Mrs. Wentworth," Sir Edward said, smiling. "My sisters keep me excellently well informed of all the latest rigs and fripperies. Many an evening I've sat in our drawing room and been caught up in a lively discussion of bonnets, pelisses, embroidered muslins and yes, long sleeves. I myself was unhappy to hear not too long ago that long sleeves are indeed become popular for evening wear.''

Clara smiled warmly at him in gratitude and Henrietta glowed with delight. Alyssa could not help but chuckle at the thought of the athletic-looking Sir Edward deep in discussion of the latest mode.

Lord Brookmere turned at the sound of her laugh, and she was surprised to find his gaze was not one of disapproval. Indeed, she felt as though she were being weighed, measured and, curiously enough, not found wanting. She was about to venture a word to him, but it seemed that her aunt was not yet satisfied to let her favorite subjects drop.

"But the prince regent?" she persisted irrepressibly. "Is he not to blame? One hears such dreadful things about all his *affaires*, and even though his wife is said to have a string of lovers, how can one really blame the poor lady if her own husband does not trouble to—''

This time Alyssa interrupted to rescue the by now truly embarrassed Sir Edward.

"Aunt Henrietta, you know that gossip of that sort is most unsuitable.'' She did not like to sound prudish, but anything less than a frank reminder would have no effect on her aunt.

"I beg to disagree with you, Miss Wentworth.''

She looked at Brookmere, startled at this wholly unexpected defense of Henrietta, whose vulgar behavior had formerly so offended him.

"If you are to sojourn in town," he continued, un-smiling except for an almost imperceptible crinkle at the corners of his mouth, "you will have to accustom yourself to hearing such talk everywhere. It is the pleasure, almost the custom, to speculate about the activities of royalty, be they moral or...otherwise." His last word was a challenge to her to contradict him.

"That may well be true, my lord," she said almost without thinking, "but although we may be forced to listen to such matters being discussed by others, our own standards of conduct do not permit us to discuss them ourselves."

Almost before she could regret giving in to the im-pulse to be so rude, he was smiling in triumph.

"Yes, I failed to consider your elevated notion of conduct." He leaned a bit closer and, under cover of the others' conversation, said softly, "No doubt the guests at your village inn are still remarking among themselves on how much your standards impressed them."

"Oh!" Alyssa fumed and bit back a sharp retort. His own conduct was infamous, and she would like nothing better than to tell him so. His grin widened, but the conversation now became general and she was forced to reply to a remark of Sir Edward's instead of whispering to his high and mighty lordship exactly what she thought of him.

By now she did not know whose fault it was that they could not have a civil conversation, and she did not much care. But she was determined that such an overbearing, conceited fellow would not have the last word, even if she had to embarrass herself again and again.

She was surprised and not a little irritated when her stepmother asked the two gentlemen to stay and share a cold luncheon with them. Sir Edward, without even consulting his friend, accepted the invitation. He was obviously very taken with Clara and wanted to continue his conversation with her, but Alyssa was sure that her stepmother had a different idea in mind. No doubt she thought that Sir Edward, and probably the Viscount Brookmere, as well, were eminently eligible and that their acquaintance should be cultivated for her stepdaughter's sake.

Sir Edward was admittedly attractive, and so amiable and courteous that no one could deny he would make an acceptable suitor, even on short acquaintance. Yet Alyssa felt no inclination to pursue him or try to fix his interest. Still, she could do much worse than marry a man like him, and she reflected that she was unlikely to do much better.

The weather was so uncommonly fine that Clara suggested they stroll in the garden while the meal was being set out. Before Alyssa could arrange it otherwise, Sir Edward, flanked by Clara and Henrietta, was being guided down to the early roses, and she found her hand on the viscount's arm. He kept to a slow pace, and by the time they had crossed the terrace and entered the shrubbery, the others were no longer within hearing.

He said in a low voice, so close that she could feel his breath on her ear, "I presume, Miss Wentworth, that your foolish monologue in the village was performed for my benefit. It was meant, of course, to teach me to restrain my tongue in the presence of ladies, no matter what my private observations might be, and to suffer complete strangers to approach me with as much familiarity as they please.''

Nonplussed by this sudden attack, she looked up into his eyes, and their startling blueness, as well as the slight contemptuous curl of his lip, almost left her speechless. She tried to pull her hand from his arm, but he swiftly brought his other hand up to cover it and keep it there.

Finding it undignified to struggle, she merely said, ''You are mistaken, my lord. It was simply meant to teach you not to form an instantaneous impression from a few words overheard by chance.''

''Was it by chance, then, that your aunt addressed her remarks in such a loud voice, not fifty paces away from me? I cannot be persuaded that she did not mean for me to hear them. I am not accustomed to such behavior from ladies, unless there is an ulterior motive. Therefore my comment, which I, at least, did not intend to be overheard, was just.''

''Yes, you have been quite sought after, haven't you?'' was Alyssa's comment. ''So much so that you cannot abide even a little innocent admiration from a simple soul like my aunt? Fear not, my lord. I assure you that no one in this household has had any ulterior motive in seeking out your acquaintance, and if we had not met by chance yesterday, you probably would never have heard of me!''

She tore her arm away and walked on briskly, though chastising herself for losing her temper yet again with someone who was obviously of consequence in London. *I shall have to become more worldly if I want to be accepted and save Finchwood,* she thought, absently pulling leaves from the boxwood as she went along. But it sickened her to think of courting the good opinion of people like Lord Brookmere, who were so unfailingly impressed with themselves and so critical of others.

She could see the others now, gathered around the roses at the end of the gravel path, and she hesitated, still plucking at the little leaves. It would not do to make an enemy of Brookmere, but her stubbornness would not allow the words of an apology to form on her tongue. The viscount, who had not increased his leisurely pace after she left him, caught up with her and took the leaves out of her hand.

"Why don't you stop torturing the shrubbery and admit that you were wrong?" he suggested, keeping her hand in his own, "You are far too pretty to look so sullen." His voice was teasing.

She tore her hand away, and not a moment too soon, for quite unexpectedly, her pulse had leaped at his touch, and a blushing confusion was mixed with her anger.

"I shall torture it if I please, sir, as it is my shrubbery," she said a little breathlessly. "And I shall not apologize, so do not think you can ply me with compliments and cajole me like one of your simpering London misses, who, no doubt, are responsible for setting you up so high in your own esteem."

Raising her head, she looked him squarely in the eye, wanting to wipe the smirk from his face. "As for my behavior yesterday, it was the result of your extreme provocation. My Aunt Henrietta is a very good woman. There is not an ill-natured bone in her body, and if she is a trifle less restrained in her manners than most, it is because she did not have the advantage of mixing with society.''

His eyes lost their look of amusement and his brows drew together. He seemed about to render a biting reply, but even this did not deter Alyssa. She met his azure gaze unblinking.

''Doubtless my aunt has told you her own romanticized version of our origins, but the simple truth is that we Wentworths come of an ancient line of . . . tradesmen. My grandfather and his before him were weavers. My father was for many years the proprietor of a successful firm dealing in the products of our looms and mills. A simple family, living well on the results of their own toil, with no inclination for elegance and artifice. Scorn us if you like, and laugh at our vulgarity if you must, but not, if you please, till you have left our property.''

With this she swept past him to join the others, too quickly to see the changes in his expression. Contempt, succeeded by surprise, followed by understanding crossed his face.

Joining her aunt in pointing out the beauties of the garden to Sir Edward, she determined not to allow the Viscount Brookmere to provoke her into saying anything more. In this she was aided by Brookmere, himself, for he addressed to her only the blandest remarks, none requiring an answer, during the whole of luncheon.

Clara was clearly delighted with the visitors and invited them to attend the Wentworths' first dinner party in town. They both accepted immediately, and Alyssa could not help feeling uneasy. Who else, she wondered, could they invite to dine with these two gentlemen of consequence? She hoped that Noddley's investigations would yield some useful information on the ton, and that Mary Carstairs would be able to introduce her to some agreeable people. At least of Mary and her husband, a young baronet, she knew that she had no need to be ashamed. But she knew no one else of fashion in London.

Her relief was extreme when the gentlemen finally left, although not before the viscount took the opportunity to murmur, "I look forward to meeting you often in town, Miss Wentworth." It was all she could do to reply with a civil tongue to this remark.

After the visitors had ridden away, Alyssa retired to her room, complaining to Clara of the headache. She sat at her window, but even the contemplation of the blue sky and feathery clouds could not help her put the Viscount Brookmere and her own behavior out of her mind.

She was ashamed of herself for being unable to control her reactions and allowing him to goad her into exposing herself to his disapproval. It was as though his very presence loosed her inhibitions and compelled her to be brutally honest. Honesty, she was worldly enough to know, would do her little good in the artificial world of society.

While Alyssa was engaged in these meditations, the subject of them was riding in companionable silence behind his friend on the road to Oakhill.

Sir Edward contemplated the view of his new home. "Daresay you're right about that roof, Charles," he said, breaking into his friend's abstraction. "I'll call in some of the local men tomorrow. And will you not let me thank you for coming to my aid? Don't know what I would do without the benefit of your experience. Still—'' he sighed, eyeing his friend's excellent riding and powerful build ''—in a way it's too bad that you were left with that old pile of yours to refurbish, and no fortune to speak of, when your father died. Just in the hottest part of the war, too. By God, you would have made a bang-up cavalry officer!''

Lord Brookmere smiled, well aware that this was one of the highest compliments his friend could bestow. He himself had long since stopped regretting the necessity that had sent his younger brother into a glorious army career, while his own fate, at the age of twenty-one, had been to do battle with debt, ruin and neglect, the legacy of their gamester father.

Ten years later, still unmarried and the despair of matchmaking mamas in both town and country, his affairs were settled and his life predictable. The Viscount Brookmere was bored.

His many interests, not limited to horses, driving four-in-hand, shooting, boxing, hunting and women, were no longer enough to keep the dreaded ennui at bay. He liked the London life of the ton, the evening parties, the theater, his clubs, and derived a wry amusement at being so sought after, when for years he had been looked upon as the reverse of desirable. But even all the sporting activities of the Corinthian and the delicately veiled invitations to intrigue with beautiful and bored married ladies failed to excite him now.

Admiration followed him everywhere. Young ladies being presented knew that his notice could raise them several levels higher in the esteem of society. Young bucks aped his manner and dress, which emulated the strictest precepts of Brummell. To a man they all envied his bang-up carriages and prime horses that were, as many an awed youngster had remarked, "complete to a shade."

All of this was very well, thought his lordship, suppressing a yawn, but it was swiftly becoming a dead bore.

"You know, Edward, in a way I miss those days when my whole fortune and future hung on a thread and I was only one step ahead of the bailiffs. Now that life is settled, it has become damnably dull!"

Sir Edward grinned. "You don't mean that, my fine fellow, not really. Why, you would be the first to complain if your life could not be just as you ordered it. Tell you what's wanted, though." He slowed his horse and leaned toward his friend. "You ought to get yourself a wife."

"I!" replied his lordship incredulously. "Rather it is you, a great fellow of five-and-thirty, a war hero with a dashing scar—*you* should be donning the knee breeches and taking yourself off to Almack's to pick yourself a likely Lady Talbot. You'd be snapped up before a month is out."

"Almack's! Not my style at all, Charles. No. In fact, I think an older lady, not a chit out of the schoolroom, would suit me much better."

"Yes, Mrs. Wentworth is very pretty, and such a sweet disposition, don't you think?"

"Oh-ho, and did you think I didn't notice how you stared at Miss Wentworth and wandered in the garden alone with her?" Sir Edward retorted. But he received no answer, for the Viscount Brookmere had spurred his mount and galloped away.

CHAPTER FIVE

THE NEXT TWO WEEKS sped by in preparation, and before Alyssa even had time to reconsider her decision to lay siege to the ton, she found herself leaving her final instructions with Rogers and directing her maid, Nan, in the packing of her gowns. That morning she had finally received a communication from Mr. Noddley, and at every spare moment during the day she reread its contents, anxious to make herself familiar with the results of the solicitor's work.

Noddley wrote of the people whose approval it was necessary to seek and the great houses to which she should strive to be invited in order to gain acceptance into the highest circles. He wrote also of the respected position of her mother's aunt, Lady Elizabeth Pomeroy, and that her mother's name had been mentioned only in whispers in society since her family had disowned her.

Alyssa was dismayed to think that the solicitor's misgivings had caused him to fail her at the last, for the focus of her plans, the list of eligible, titled gentlemen, was missing from his letter. But a brief postscript, assuring her that he had not forgotten the other part of the business, made her realize that she had much to learn from Mr. Noddley's caution and discretion. It was too delicate a matter to be handled by mail. She resigned herself to waiting until her arrival in London before being able to view the list.

The trip to town was uneventful, if tiring. The Wentworths arrived in Green Street by late afternoon of the second day of their journey, drawing up before the elegant, three-story brick town house, with its wrought-iron fence and brightly painted door. The polished brass knocker had just been put back in place, signifying that the family was back in residence.

In spite of Alyssa's stiffness and weariness as she descended from the carriage, she was immediately infected with all the excitement and anticipation that a visit to the city usually generated. This visit, she knew, was of far greater importance than her previous trips, made with her father and stepmother for the purpose of sight-seeing, shopping and the theater. Now, Alyssa thought with a shiver of fear, her entire future hung on the results of a few weeks of determined socializing.

Crossing the threshold into the hall, Alyssa reflected that at least no one need have any hesitation about accepting the Wentworths' hospitality. She was sure the town house was every bit as commodious and elegantly appointed as that of the most fashionable leader of society. The sweeping oak and iron staircases, the lofty drawing rooms with their gilt and decorated mantels and ceilings, and the excellent cooking of Mrs. Oliver, who even included a few French dishes in her repertoire, would satisfy even the highest stickler.

THE NEXT MORNING Henrietta led the way on a grand shopping expedition. The ladies visited modistes, milliners, warehouses and shoemakers and viewed so many styles and made so many purchases that at length Alyssa declared herself too exhausted to move. She returned to their carriage while Clara accompanied Henrietta into one last shop, with little hope of dissuading her from the purchase of a hideous fringed shawl of a bright pea green to accent her new cerise-striped walking dress.

Seated in the barouche, Alyssa was impatient to be home, impatient for the next day, for she expected a call from Mr. Noddley. Now that she was so close to putting her plan into practice, she was beginning to feel apprehension about the wisdom of it. Rapt in thought, staring sightlessly over the coachman's shoulder, she was utterly at a loss when a deep voice at her side broke into her reverie.

"Good day, Miss Wentworth. I have been wondering when I would see you in town."

"Oh!" Alyssa's eyes widened in astonishment.

Lord Brookmere, mounted on a flawless gray hack, had appeared at the side of the barouche and was now observing her reaction with amusement.

Alyssa struggled to regain her composure and nodded politely. "As you see, I am here," she commented, managing a tone of serene indifference.

His lordship was not a whit disturbed by her coolness. "I had hoped to see you and the other ladies at Almack's last night, but I was disappointed."

She looked up quickly from beneath her lashes and saw that he was smiling. Insufferable!

"No doubt," she replied, looking straight at the back of the coachman's interested head. Almack's, indeed! Why, he must know that they could never have procured vouchers so soon, if indeed it were possible at all.

"Then perhaps I shall see you at Lady Jersey's card party? Or Lady Allerton's ball Friday next?" he taunted.

It was becoming more difficult to keep her face expressionless. If only they were not in a public place, Alyssa fumed, she would tell this arrogant lord exactly what she thought of him. As it was, she could only stare at him with fury in her eyes and shake her head with as much dignity as she could assume. How dared he amuse himself at the idea of her ambiguous social position!

"Pity," was all he said in reply, but he retreated a little from the blaze his teasing had kindled in those emerald eyes.

Alyssa was unable to control herself a moment longer, and her throat was tight with the urge to shout at him.

"It is indeed a pity," she said icily, "when a man of your stature must resort to mockery of a lady for his own amusement."

"I assure you, I do not mock," retorted Brookmere, irritated at her having taken him so seriously. "What is so odd, after all, in a beautiful young heiress being seen to shine in society? Perhaps it is you who find the idea a mockery."

"If all the gentlemen in London are as rude as you, my lord," she said, "then perhaps I would be happier staying in the country. But before long, sir, whether you think it likely or not, the Wentworths will appear at Almack's and anywhere else that your kind are welcome." She stopped, horrified at saying so much.

To complete her embarrassment, he only laughed. "Very well, Miss Wentworth. Almack's it is, but pray don't forget to save a dance for me—perhaps a waltz? I'm sure a young lady of your ingenuity would find not only a way to get vouchers, but to obtain permission to waltz, as well. Good day."

He rode away before she could choke out another word. *And it was just as well,* she reflected a few minutes later as Henrietta and Clara joined her. She would have said something very rude. She only hoped that Lord Brookmere was not the kind of gentleman who liked to spread gossip. If so, her chances would be ruined before she had begun, for surely he would have a dozen unkind things to say about her.

Thus she would have been amazed to learn that Lord Brookmere was better amused than he had been in a fortnight. Had anyone asked him about the unknown Miss Wentworth newly come to town, the dozen things he could say would mostly have to do with the exquisite charms of tawny tresses, coral lips and sparkling green eyes.

The ladies rode home amid their packages, pleasantly tired and anticipating a good lunch and the delivery the next week of their new gowns that, Henrietta assured them, would quite cast all the other ladies in the shade. Alyssa was very quiet in the face of Henrietta's high spirits and Clara's more subdued enjoyment. She did not mention her meeting with the Viscount Brookmere.

In their absence cards had been left by Mary Carstairs as well as Sir Edward Talbot and his sisters. There was also a note from Mr. Noddley, and Alyssa tore it open eagerly. The solicitor would call upon her the next day, presumably with the list. Her heart began to pound and she clenched the scrap of paper in her hand. Then her job would begin in earnest. But she told herself she would not be frightened, and sent off a message asking Noddley to call in the morning, so that afterward she could pay a visit to Mary, and perhaps the Talbots, as well.

It would not do to neglect the good-natured Sir Edward, who seemed either not to know or not to care about the origins of the Wentworth family. She only hoped he would not have his friend Lord Brookmere with him. In fact, she told herself, everything would be so much easier if the viscount would ignore her existence altogether. But recalling his casual mockery, she had not a hope that he would.

MR. NODDLEY, when he met the ladies the next day, had little to add to what he had written in his letter to Alyssa at Finchwood, at least not in the presence of Henrietta and Clara.

"Aside from the people I have already mentioned to you, Miss Wentworth," he said, easing himself onto a settee in the morning room, "there are few others whom it would be worth your while to cultivate. One of the patronesses of Almack's, to be sure. It is imperative that you be seen there, and none of those very particular ladies will grant vouchers to anyone they do not find acceptable."

It was no more than Alyssa had expected, but Henrietta and Clara looked discouraged at this. Even her lively aunt was not so optimistic as to suppose that the family of a tradesman who had been party to a scandalous mésalliance would be found acceptable.

The solicitor, however, was more sanguine. "I believe you should apply for assistance to your friend Mrs. Carstairs, as I have heard that her husband is a distant connection of Lady Jersey. Perhaps he can introduce you to her."

He advised the ladies for some moments more and then turned to Alyssa. "I have some other, er, matters concerning the estate to discuss with you, my dear. Perhaps the ladies will excuse us, for we need not bore them with the trivial and uninteresting details...."

His look said exactly the opposite, and Alyssa felt her heart quicken again. She was about to learn the results of his researches. Suppressing her eagerness, she excused herself and the solicitor as calmly as she could, but she felt Henrietta's curious glance and Clara's concerned one on them as they left the room.

"Well, Mr. Noddley?" Alyssa asked, fixing an expectant look on his face when once they were alone.

Now he seemed uncertain, and muttered something to himself as he reluctantly withdrew a folded paper from his waistcoat pocket. He turned it over in his hands and it was all Alyssa could do not to snatch it away.

"I still feel in my bones that we are making a dreadful mistake, but ..." He sighed and handed her the paper.

As she scanned the list, Alyssa noted with disappointment that it contained only six names, three of them already familiar to her, and the sight of one of them brought a blush to her cheeks. Though undoubtedly there were many unmarried gentlemen of the ton, Noddley was probably trying to protect her by narrowing the choice to the safest and most unobjectionable six he could find. He could not know that one of them was quite objectionable, indeed.

He stood watching her, his little blue eyes blinking rapidly.

"I know three of these gentlemen already," she told him. "Lord Robert Norton is the uncle of James Carstairs and, from what Mary has told me, is a confirmed bachelor."

"Yes, but it seems that his lordship has had some recent losses. He had a run of poor luck in some speculative investing, which was rather foolish of him, for he knows nothing of business, but, then again, he depends on Fosby, who as everyone knows, is one of the worst—"

"Yes, Mr. Noddley," Alyssa interrupted impatiently, "I quite understand. And I understand why Sir Edward Talbot is the next name on the list, for having met him, I thought he was perfectly decent and amiable, though I know nothing of his financial affairs."

"Oh, only the slightest difficulty there," he informed her. "As you probably know, his new lands and the house need considerable attention, which will cost quite a bit. And he, I am afraid, is not immune to the lure of faro and hazard, though having lost a large sum, he has wisely cut back on his play."

"But what I simply do not understand," Alyssa said, unable to control herself any longer, "is how can you possibly imagine that Lord Brookmere, of all people, would ever show an interest in me? Why, from the moment we met it has been the most horrid, embarrassing—"

She broke off hastily, knowing that she could never confess to the solicitor her foolishness at her first meeting, indeed at all her meetings with the viscount.

"What I mean is, we have not dealt well together from the first, and I am convinced we should not suit." She smoothed some infinitesimal wrinkles in her skirt with one hand and clenched the other, with the list in it.

The solicitor's eyes were full of disappointment. "I'm sorry you feel that way, my dear," he said, surprised at her vehemence, "for he seemed to me the most eligible of the six. Of course, he is not precisely in need of a fortune, but from what I was able to learn of him, he is not the man to marry on a mere romantical whim. On the contrary, he has shown himself to be completely practical, knowing and awake upon every suit. And if you will forgive my presumption—" his broad face reddened "—he has the reputation of being susceptible to a pretty face and figure. The combination of fortune and beauty could prove the undoing of his bachelorhood, which has been frustrating the ladies of the ton these ten years."

"I doubt, my dear Mr. Noddley," said Alyssa with dignity, "that the illustrious viscount would stoop to offer for a mere merchant's daughter. You are too prejudiced in my favor to see how unlikely it would be."

"Miss Wentworth, you will have to learn to value yourself higher," replied the old man affectionately, "for Lord Mannerly is the second son of a duke, Lord Selbridge is an earl and even Lord Lynwood is a marquess. Why, Brookmere is the least of them!"

Alyssa sighed. "Very well, then, who are all these high-ranking gentlemen and why do you think they would condescend to consider me as a prospective bride?"

Noddley launched into a report on the fruits of his research. "John Lynwood is an accepted, but admittedly eccentric member of the ton. It seems he has spent most of his youth and almost all his fortune in mounting scientific expeditions to outlandish places to study the flora and fauna. Now the word is that he has come home to marry for the purpose of honoring his title with an heir and, incidentally, to rebuild his fortune. He is reported to be forty, handsome and quite intelligent."

Not altogether entranced by this description, Alyssa bade him continue.

"Lord Mannerly is rather young—he only reaches his majority next year, when he will come into a tidy property from his mother. Just now his papa keeps a tight hand on the purse strings, and it is common knowledge that though his lordship is singularly free of the usual gentleman's vices, he *is* rather extravagant when it comes to his wardrobe and his art collection. Everyone expects him to look first for fortune when seeking a wife."

"And the earl?" inquired Alyssa, beginning to think better of her plan, for neither of these gentlemen sounded agreeable.

"Ah, Selbridge!" The solicitor rubbed his hands together. "A fine young man, from all I've been able to gather, at present in some financial distress. He has just undertaken the addition of a new wing to the ancestral home and the expense is temporarily overwhelming. Most say he has been quite ready to marry and set up his nursery these two years, but he has found no one to suit him.''

Alyssa rose from her chair and went to take the solicitor's hand. ''Mr. Noddley, however can I thank you for your kindness and loyalty? I am sure that without your help I could do nothing but lose my last chance to inherit.''

''Nonsense, child, your papa was a good friend. It's the least I can do,'' he mumbled.

''But tell me,'' she went on, ''however did you manage to discover such things about all these gentlemen?''

''Experience, my dear, years of it, has provided me with many a useful acquaintance. A little chat, a glass or two of wine . . . one can find out almost anything if only one knows the proper way to go about it.'' He winked at her conspiratorially.

She smiled, but as he prepared to leave, stopped him.

''Please, take the list with you,'' she said, pressing it into his hand. ''I should hate to misplace it or have Clara or my aunt find it. I'm sure it will be much safer locked away in your office with all our legal papers.''

''Certainly, my dear. Oh, and if you find yourself short of the ready, just send word to me, and I shall set you up with enough to keep you in frills and fripperies until one of these gentlemen obliges you,'' he said playfully. ''I know how much it costs these days to live in style, and since you are making an attempt in good faith to comply with the terms of the will, I'm sure the estate can advance you any reasonable sum.''

She thanked him again and bid him good-day, her mind full of the men on the list and what she would do when she met them, for meet them she would.

CHAPTER SIX

ALYSSA HAD NOT SEEN Mary Carstairs for several months and was eager to have the benefit of her advice. But she wondered, as she was ushered into the sitting room of the Carstairs' town house on Mount Street, just how much she ought to confide in her. In her first note she had merely said that she, her aunt and stepmother were planning an extended stay in London and would be pleased if Mary could introduce them to some congenial people.

Alyssa decided that she must at least tell Mary about the terms of her father's will, but that she would keep the full extent of her plans to herself. Mary would be horrified if she were to confess that she was determined to select her husband in such a cold and calculating manner.

These worries were forgotten in the joyous reunion of the two ladies. Mrs. Carstairs was of a height with her friend, but her hair was a lovely chestnut color and she had eyes of deep brown. She was dressed fashionably, but modestly, and Alyssa remembered of old Mary's reluctance to attract attention to herself. It was her sweetness of disposition, her intelligence and gentle manners that had won the heart of James Carstairs.

In a few minutes Alyssa had made her friend familiar with her situation, and Mary's horror at the revelation of the conditions of her inheritance made her glad she had decided not to say anything further.

"How dreadful for you! Especially when all these years you had no suspicion of it." She leaned forward and patted her friend's hand encouragingly. "Well," she said firmly, "it will not signify, for I can help you to meet a great many people, and in no time at all we shall have you married to a wonderful man and we can be two matrons together."

Alyssa hugged her gratefully, glowing in the warmth of Mary's determined optimism and support, but she knew it could not possibly be so simple. However, she listened eagerly as her friend began to outline her prospective social calendar.

"We attend a great many parties, as well as the theater and the opera, and Almack's, of course—oh, we must see about getting vouchers for you—and though we are not on visiting terms with the true cream of the ton, there are several gentlemen of our acquaintance whom you might wish to meet."

Alyssa thanked her warmly and asked after her husband.

"Oh, James is as attentive as ever, and people laugh at us behind their hands because we are so unfashionably in love! He spends more time with his wife and less time at his club than any man in London. Still, I do love it when we can be alone together in the country."

Mary paused, and a secret smile crossed her face. "No one knows yet but James and our parents, but I am increasing and hope to be mother by November."

"Dear Mary, how wonderful!"

"But don't worry," Mary continued, "it is not so far advanced yet that I will not be able to show you a magnificent time. First I'll give a dinner, just a dozen people or so, to start you off. Oh, and as soon as I got your note, I obtained cards for all three of you to Mrs. Allingham's rout on Thursday, and on Saturday there is a Venetian breakfast—"

Alyssa stopped her with a laugh. "I can see that the easiest thing to do would be to leave my entire social life in your capable hands. I really do appreciate it, and of course I plan to reciprocate as soon as I am able."

She told Mary of becoming acquainted with her new neighbor, Sir Edward Talbot, and suggested that she might like to accompany the Wentworth ladies that day on their call. "As soon as I have enough people to form a guest list, there will be dinners, card parties and perhaps even a ball in Green Street—"

"And then," Mary interrupted, "some delightful man will offer for you and your worries will be over. Ugh, that horrid Mr. Basking! I met him at Almack's once and it gave me the shivers just to have him take my hand. No matter what happens," she added, looking earnestly at Alyssa, "you must promise never to consider marrying him. Although he is received everywhere, he has an evil reputation. You could never be happy married to such a creature. Even Finchwood and a dozen fortunes would not be worth the sacrifice."

Alyssa, without promising anything, assured her that it was unlikely she would become so desperate as to consider it, but privately she was not so sure.

The visit to the Talbots later that day seemed to indicate less difficulty in being accepted by the ton than Alyssa had expected. Whether they had never heard about the scandal of twenty years ago, or of her father's lowly origins, she had no idea, but Sir Edward's sisters, Julia and Beatrice, were not at all standoffish with the Wentworth ladies.

They were elegant but pleasant girls whose fine airs were merely a thin veneer over kind, lively and gossipy characters. Confronted by Aunt Henrietta in all her plumage, they did not so much as giggle behind their hands, and they took special pains to get to know Clara, while Sir Edward looked on with pleasure.

Before the end of the visit the Talbots had accepted an invitation to tea at the Wentworths' along with Mary Carstairs, whom they had not known before but whom they received very kindly. Clara was engaged to drive in the park with Sir Edward the following afternoon. She had hesitated before accepting this invitation, and had sought her stepdaughter's eyes, but Alyssa had smiled and nodded encouragement. Despite Sir Edward's presence on Mr. Noddley's list, she could tell that the former officer was far too taken with her stepmother to have a glance to spare for her, so she consigned him to Clara's care with no regrets.

"And how is your good friend Lord Brookmere, Sir Edward?" Henrietta wanted to know, in between unladylike gulps of ratafia and a mouthful of biscuits.

"Well, thanks to him, I was able to dispatch my business at Oakhill much more quickly than anticipated. I'm sure that I couldn't be more surprised than you ladies must be to see me here so soon." He grinned. "Ignorant as I was, I thought it would take at least a month, but Brookmere assured me it could all be arranged in a fortnight, so—"

The Talbot's butler appeared in the doorway, and right behind him was the subject of Sir Edward's remarks. Alyssa swallowed hastily and tried to hold back a fit of choking as Lord Brookmere, shaking the hand of his friend, let his gaze wander over the room to fasten on her.

Greetings and introductions made, Lord Brookmere settled in a chair much too close to Alyssa for her own comfort, and she was hard put not to scowl when Mary raised her eyebrows encouragingly at the sight.

"And how goes the season for the illustrious Wentworth family?" he inquired in a voice low enough so that only Alyssa could hear. "Have the harridans who rule society admitted you to their charmed circle?"

"Whatever do you mean?" Alyssa could not keep the irritation from her voice.

His eyes were an opaque blue in the dim, half-shuttered room, and his lips curved in amusement. "That is why you came to town, is it not, Miss Wentworth? Why, I wonder, this sudden interest in London, when to my very good knowledge none of your family has ever expressed an interest in the approval of society?"

Annoyance, and embarrassment that Mr. Noddley had actually placed this insufferable man on his list of prospective husbands, made her lash out at him, though she had promised herself she would behave no matter what the provocation.

"My reasons, sir, are none of your affair. A lady can come to London for the season if she pleases, I suppose, without exciting any vulgar curiosity." Her tone dripped scorn and her glance challenged him.

He leaned a little closer, and she could smell the fragrance of his light, herbal cologne and freshly laundered linen, overlaid with a sharp and indefinable masculine scent.

"Certainly, but it cannot help but rouse my curiosity when a young lady of your background, recently bereaved, descends upon London suddenly, with family in tow, obviously determined to enter a society that was previously closed to her."

Alyssa was shocked at his knowledge. "How do you know any of this?" she demanded.

Brookmere lounged gracefully in his chair and stretched out his well-shaped legs. "Surely, Miss Wentworth, you must realize that your sudden appearance in town, though you have not yet made your presence felt in the social round, has stirred up curiosity and the memory of an old scandal."

Alyssa flinched at the mention of it, although his voice was matter-of-fact. She had been afraid of this, but she could not, would not, let the opinions of society deter her from her plan of action.

"Perhaps," she replied with studied indifference. "But my reasons are no different from anyone else's."

For a moment, Brookmere simply gazed at her.

"I see," he murmured finally. "Well, whatever your reasons, I wish you good fortune." He straightened and bowed slightly in his chair, then turned to converse with Julia Talbot, who sat next to him and had been listening eagerly.

Alyssa was left to wonder what he could possibly have meant by his last remark. Could he have some notion of her real purpose in coming to town? But, no, not even her closest family knew the full extent of her plans. Nevertheless, she was, as always, uneasy in his presence and was relieved when he rose to take his leave, with the excuse that he had to prepare for a journey into the country.

He gave Alyssa an ironical bow and an infuriating half smile as he bade her goodbye. She simply nodded in return, happy that he was leaving town and hoping he would stay away a good long time.

"Going to visit with the Beddoes," she heard Sir Edward say to Clara. "They hardly come to town, have a large house party every year, always invite Brookmere. But I suspect that we will be receiving an interesting announcement from that quarter this year, eh, my dears?"

He winked at his sisters, who smiled slyly and reminded him in whispered tones that nothing had been announced yet. Nevertheless, they looked as though they were in expectation of an interesting bit of gossip to distribute any day.

None of the Wentworth ladies had any idea of what this could mean. Alyssa puzzled over it for some time, until on the way home, Mary said, "the *on-dit* is that Lord Brookmere is going to offer for the earl of Beddoe's daughter. He's known the family for ages, and she's quite young—barely seventeen."

Two out of six, mused Alyssa after bidding her friend goodbye at her door. Not that it was any great loss to her. List or no list, she would never consider Lord Brookmere as a husband. The earl's daughter was welcome to him.

A FORTNIGHT FILLED more and more with social events of all kinds passed almost too swiftly for Alyssa. Although delighted at the surprising welcome she received from Mary's friends and acquaintances, she was hard put to attach names to faces, so many were there.

There were a few malicious people who ventured to comment on her origins and declined an introduction, but it was done very subtly. The younger people in general did not give a fig for the twenty-year-old scandal and accepted Alyssa unreservedly. Yet she had still not been presented to any of the true arbiters of fashion, or introduced into the most exclusive circles, and there was no question, of course, of being presented at court.

Another worry was their failure to obtain vouchers for Almack's. The only chance would be in getting the nod of approval from Lady Jersey. But so far James Carstairs had not been able to arrange a meeting between his distant cousin and the Wentworth ladies. Adding to Alyssa's distress was the fact that she had so far met only one of the other gentlemen on Noddley's list.

Lord Robert Norton had been introduced to her at a dinner given by the Carstairs, and by chance Alyssa had been his dinner partner. He was a short, heavyset man of some forty years, who looked older. He had a sad, brooding air about him, and contributed little to the conversation, though he did not precisely neglect Alyssa.

His speech, which was not distinguished by anything particularly sensible or interesting, was punctuated by so many sighs and long swallows of wine that soon Alyssa was happy to leave him to the attentions of her aunt, who sat at his other side. Unlike her niece, she appeared intrigued by his tragic demeanor.

When the gentlemen rejoined the ladies in the drawing room after partaking of their port, Alyssa was amused to see Lord Norton immediately seek out her aunt and remain at her side for the rest of the evening. Apparently the plump little lady in the shocking violet gown and peacock blue turban entertained rather than irritated this taciturn gentleman, for Alyssa could swear that she actually saw him smile as Henrietta chattered away.

Since she had rejected him as a possible husband from the start, Alyssa was not at all put out. Indeed, she was only too happy to have her aunt safely occupied where she could not make any embarrassing remarks in the general company.

So far it seemed that Lord Brookmere had not returned to town, and Alyssa took this as a sign that the rumored betrothal was becoming a settled thing. What else could keep a gentleman so in demand away from the activities of the season?

Henrietta, who had an alert ear for gossip, reported one day that it was now common knowledge that his name was linked with that of the earl of Beddoe's daughter. "Why, the girl is not yet out, and all the other gentlemen are planning to take his lordship to task for getting the jump on them. They say he is quite taken with the child," she prattled on, "although some of them are unkind enough to say it is only her fortune that attracts him. Did you know that he was almost ruined, when he first came into the title, on account of his papa's having lost the fortune at hazard? Lord Robert says they are laying odds at White's whether the heiress will have him, or wait till her come-out and pluck a plumper bird than a mere viscount.''

Alyssa's curiosity had been satisfied, but she was strangely irritated at this news. "It is beyond everything that a man's every movement should be known and discussed by all and sundry. Surely the Viscount Brookmere's plans are of no concern to anyone but himself.''

"But his lordship is so popular," protested her aunt, "everything he does is of interest to society.''

"Well, it is certainly of no interest to me," retorted Alyssa.

"Yes," said Clara knowingly, "you and he did not seem to get on very well together.''

"Nothing of the kind." Alyssa turned away so that her stepmother could not see her face.

Clara wisely did not respond and hushed Henrietta when she would have continued to sing the viscount's praises.

Alyssa thought of her dwindling list and, strangely, of the unexpected touch of his lordship's hand on hers and of the clean scent that came back to her nostrils at the thought of him. He had told her once that she was too pretty to be sullen. Did he really think her pretty, or was that just the way of a man of the world trying to get around a resistant female? Determined not to care, she put on her new leghorn bonnet with the coral satin riband, picked up her yellow kid gloves, and sallied forth on a round of morning calls.

CHAPTER SEVEN

AT LONG LAST there came word of James Carstairs's success with Lady Jersey, and the Wentworth ladies were honored with a morning call from one Lady Marchinton, in the name of that august patroness.

Mary's eyes gleamed with amusement. "She means to make a visit of inspection," she warned Alyssa the evening before the call was to take place, "to see if you are fit to talk and dance with the cream of society in the stuffiest set of rooms imaginable."

Alyssa could not find anything to laugh at. "I beg of you, Mary, do not make sport of me. Of course, we have met a great many people, but you know as well as I do, to Almack's I must go, or—"

"Pooh," scoffed her friend. "There is not a thing to worry about. Your appearance and deportment speak for themselves, and even Lady Marchinton, with her sharp little eyes, will not be able to detect anything that would disqualify you and Clara from being admitted to the assembly rooms."

"And Aunt Henrietta?" Alyssa inquired.

"Well..." Mary hesitated. "Perhaps," she continued with a smile, "it would be as well if you encouraged her to be away from the house tomorrow morning."

So it was with relief that Alyssa saw Henrietta off to several appointments for fittings and some shopping the next morning. She fully expected her aunt to be out till afternoon.

Lady Marchinton was a haughty little woman with a very erect posture and a thin, pointed face. Graciously allowing herself to be presented to Clara, to whom she merely gave a frigid nod, and acknowledging with a single word the presence of Mrs. Carstairs, she consented to be seated on a striped silk sofa. From this position she surveyed the room through a silver-mounted quizzing glass for a long time.

Alyssa avoided her friend's eyes for fear that she would giggle, but, after a tense silence, expressed her gratitude for her ladyship's condescension in paying a call on such rank newcomers to society.

Lady Marchinton regarded her sternly. "You ought to be grateful, Miss Wentworth. It is not often that the patronesses interest themselves in persons of a certain background. But my good friend Lady Jersey has kindly consented to consider you."

Alyssa forced herself to swallow her pride at the insulting reference to her father's business. Think only of Finchwood, she told herself, of Finchwood . . . and of Henry Basking. Then she replied as mildly as she could while Clara rang for refreshments to be brought.

Alyssa was grateful for Mary's presence, for without any apparent effort, her normally shy friend took upon herself the burden of introducing a new topic of conversation. By the time the sherry and biscuits had arrived, her ladyship had unbent slightly. Indeed, she went so far as to compliment Alyssa on the decor of the room and to assert, albeit in a disappointed tone, that she saw no reason why Alyssa and her chaperons should not receive vouchers.

Alyssa breathed a quiet sigh of relief and exchanged a little smile with Clara. But in the next second she knew she had been premature, for a bustle in the hall announced the untimely arrival of her aunt. Henrietta, in one of her more outrageous morning gowns of turquoise with lime green trimming, entered the drawing room unceremoniously, calling loudly for her niece and sister-in-law.

"La, my dears, and just who do you think I met in Pall Mall? Why, no one but Mrs. Morrat, with dear Serena and Hester. They were just across the way, and I said to myself, I must not let them pass by without seeing me, so I called out as loud as I could and gave my parcel to Gage so I could wave both my hands, and sure enough, they saw me!"

Blind to the warning glances of Clara and Alyssa, she rambled on about her old friends, while Lady Marchinton looked on, all disgust and astonishment. Alyssa's heart sank to her slippers and it was some minutes before Clara finally directed Henrietta's attention to the fact that they had a guest.

"Oh, why, your ladyship!" Henrietta stared openmouthed at the pale and frowning visitor. "Such an honor—I daresay you're the one as is come about the vouchers? I do so want to attend—although I fear that my late brother William, dear Alyssa's papa, would not approve. He used to say that any place that could be so particular as to membership could get along very well without him. But, then, gentlemen never do understand, do they?"

During this spate of friendly chat, she had approached Lady Marchinton and, taking a hand that was by no means offered to her, pumped it in a friendly way.

Her ladyship extricated her hand, an angry flush mounting to her lined forehead. She opened her mouth and swiftly closed it again, as if there were no possible reply to this.

Alyssa, Clara and Mary were in agonies, but before any of them could speak, Henrietta had planted herself on the sofa beside the visitor. Leaning confidingly toward her, she said, "Such a man was William Wentworth! There was never his like nor will be again, and why people were so unkind as to cut Alyssa's poor mama when he married her, I'm sure I will never understand!"

This was more than enough for her ladyship. Rising stiffly, so that not a thread of her gown brushed against Henrietta's, she said, "Indeed, I fear you most certainly would not," in her most scornful accents and sailed out of the room.

Alyssa followed, her highest hopes dashed to the ground. As soon as they were out of the drawing room, Lady Marchinton turned to her. "Pray, do not, Miss Wentworth, attempt any explanation. For a moment I was convinced that your family had escaped the hint of vulgarity by which most of our mercantile class distinguish their behavior, but that creature who calls herself your aunt does nothing to recommend you to our favor. No doubt the friends she spoke of would wish to receive the entrée along with you." She visibly suppressed a shudder at the thought. "No, I shall advise Lady Jersey to withhold the vouchers. Good day.''

Before Alyssa could begin the stinging reply she had been preparing at such an insult, her ladyship had descended the stair, just as Mary emerged from the drawing room.

Alyssa was white and trembling with anger. Her first impulse was to race down the stairs and bar the door till Lady Marchinton heard what she had to say, but Mary took her arm and held her back.

''Oh, my poor dear, I am so sorry! Whoever would have believed that it could all turn about that way in five minutes? We must not tell Henrietta what her untimely entrance cost you, for I am persuaded she would blame herself forever.''

Alyssa relaxed her tense shoulders. Quarreling with Lady Marchinton would simply add coals to the fire. She squeezed Mary's hand gratefully. ''You are such a dear friend. Anyone else would have been busy condemning poor Aunt Henrietta for her behavior, but you realize, as I do, that the dear soul cannot help being what she is. I can't say I'm entirely sorry, though. I don't believe I could have stood another moment of that awful old woman's inspection. Aunt Henrietta saved me the trouble of being civil to her for ten more minutes.''

''No, you are really too good, Alyssa,'' Mary protested with a smile. ''You must at least be allowed to regret such a misfortune.''

''Oh, I shall cry on my pillow, by and by,'' Alyssa assured her, only half jesting.

''And then,'' said Mary firmly, ''I shall ask James to approach Lady Jersey once more, to explain, and perhaps she will see you herself, instead of sending her flunky. Or maybe,'' she said a bit more uncertainly, ''I shall have a word with Countess Lieven herself the next time I visit the assembly rooms. I'm sure she knew your mother and perhaps she will consent to admit you for her sake.''

''Perhaps,'' Alyssa agreed, with little hope.

BUT AFTER THREE DAYS during which she enjoyed dinners, dances and opera parties hardly at all, her worry over the vouchers was relieved from a most unexpected source.

Mary Carstairs called early one morning as Alyssa was finishing her breakfast. Declining offers of refreshment, Mary seated herself and fanned her face with a napkin.

''Just let me catch my breath a moment. I almost ran up the steps to tell you the good news.''

''What good news? Come, now, don't tease. You may breathe later.''

Mary looked sly. ''Well, if you can't guess…just be sure you keep Wednesday night open, or if you have engagements, cancel them.''

''Do you mean—''

''Success is ours! Would you believe that despite the horrid things that Marchinton woman told Lady Jersey about you, you are granted vouchers for Almack's. Not only you and Clara, but Henrietta, as well.''

Alyssa could only gape at her. ''How can it be?'' she finally managed to ask, between surprise and delight.

''It is most curious, and rather funny. It seems that long ago, Lady Marchinton quarreled with Countess

Lieven, over some trifle to be sure, but the affair ended in their becoming confirmed enemies. When the countess heard Lady Jersey's objections to your being admitted, and was apparently treated to a word by word description of the scene here that morning, she laughed and said that anyone who Lucy Marchinton considered vulgar was probably unexceptionable company. Have you ever heard the like?''

When she had done laughing at this odd but lucky turn of events, Alyssa only hoped that the scene between Henrietta and Lady Marchinton would not be retailed among all the latter's acquaintance. It would be difficult enough to make the right impression at Almack's without having yet more gossip precede her.

This uneasiness dogged her up till the time she was making her first curtsy to the patronesses the next evening. Despite her anxiety, she could not help but feel the excitement of what was her true debut, though she found the rooms to be not as impressive as she had expected nor so fine.

Though none of the high-ranking social arbiters of the assembly rooms looked very pleased to welcome Alyssa and her party, none of them indicated any disappointment in her manners or dress. Their reception of Henrietta was another matter.

Even Countess Lieven, who had bestowed a kind smile on Alyssa and told her she was very like her mother, seemed to regret her hastiness in rejecting her enemy's decision when she glimpsed the gown of violet *gros de Naples*, with its blue gauze petticoat and bright yellow ruching, and the outrageous feathered turban strung with beads. Surely, Alyssa thought in a second of amusement, her ladyship had not realized that she would be extending her approval to a female who resembled nothing so much as an exotic bird.

Fortunately her aunt was too excited to be hurt by the prim nods and icy glances, and did not see the dozens of quizzing glasses raised to astounded eyes as she entered the room. Alyssa did, and tried not to blush for her.

She herself drew nothing but admiration in her gown of white crepe, with its rose-pink netted tunic, the low bodice trimmed with delicate embroidery, matching that on the tiny puffed sleeves and swirling hem.

The gown set off the perfection of her arms and shoulders, and she wore a double strand of pearls, a delicate pearl-and-diamond bracelet and tiny pearls in her ears. With sweet-smelling pink flowers in her hair, she drew the gentlemen like honeybees, and soon she had been introduced to at least a dozen, who crowded round her, determined to secure a dance with this charming new entry in the marriage stakes.

While she was meeting all these potential suitors and given approval to waltz by a gratified Countess Lieven, Alyssa failed to notice the small commotion at the other end of the room. There, a foppishly bedecked Henry Basking was remarking in a loud voice to an elderly lady, "Such a to-do about this girl! But, then, one can expect nothing better than such a vulgar display from the daughter of a common tradesman."

Lady Elizabeth Pomeroy was becoming increasingly irritated at being the forced recipient of Henry Basking's poisonous remarks. She had already heard the rumor that her grandniece, daughter of her favorite niece, would be at Almack's that evening. She had stirred herself from Portman Square in order that she might see what ruin an injection of mercantile blood had wrought on the pure strain of her family.

Now, as Basking attempted to take her arm and lead her across the room, she angrily shook him off. "Keep your hands to yourself, jackanapes, and don't presume to influence your betters. I know perfectly well who the gel is and before you started jawing at me I was on my way to see her for myself. And stop goggling at me, looby. Hasn't anyone ever told you it makes you look like a demmed bullfrog?"

He dropped her arm abruptly and, turning an unbecoming shade of purple, left the old lady to continue her solitary, stately progress down the room. As one of the grand dames of the ton, Lady Pomeroy acknowledged automatically the respectful bows and greetings, her mind on this unknown young relation of hers. Though the girl's mother had been her favorite, she'd been unable to persuade her niece's parents to accept their daughter's runaway marriage to Mr. Wentworth. To keep the family peace, Lady Pomeroy had desisted after her few, unsuccessful attempts to contact her niece.

She reached the edge of the little group surrounding Alyssa and scattered them without compunction. "You, coxcomb, out of my way! Allow an old lady to pass. Bunch of mooncalves. Men aren't men anymore, and in my day the likes of you wouldn't get within a mile of this place. And *that* demmed manmilliner—" she jerked her silver head at Henry Basking, who was trying to efface himself while still maintaining a position close enough to observe everything "—that one would be drummed out of town!"

Alyssa looked up as her beaux scattered, and found herself confronted by an older and more forbidding version of her mother. She was shocked into silence for a moment. It had not occurred to her that her great-aunt, for of course this was who it must be, would seek her out in so public a place.

"Well," demanded the old lady, "what have you got to say to your aunt, gel? Nothing? You don't look like one of those whey-faced chits with not a word to say for themselves."

Alyssa could not imagine what response was called for in such a situation, but she curtsied and said frankly, "It is a great surprise to me, ma'am, to meet someone of my mother's family. I had not hoped to be recognized, as of course I am aware of the circumstances of her leaving them. But it is a real pleasure to make your acquaintance, my lady."

Lady Pomeroy sniffed, but looked pleased and said, "You may call me 'Aunt Elizabeth,' as your mama used to. I never really forgave your grandparents for what they did to her. She was a gel of spirit. You're like her," she said gruffly.

Suddenly she noticed that all conversation in the vicinity had ceased. "Get those waggling ears back in your heads, the lot of you!" she said, scowling. "No manners these days. Having a family discussion. Get along with you!"

The people began to disperse, afraid of her ladyship's temper and her renowned tongue, but they kept their eyes on the scene and whispered fiercely among themselves. Henry Basking's original plan to revive the scandal of the Wentworth's marriage had apparently succeeded, for nothing else was talked of for the rest of the evening.

And if a few fastidious gentlemen did not return to join the group around Alyssa, the report of her father's low birth did nothing to discourage the less particular ones. They realized that, though a fortune made in trade was not really quite the thing, no one being dunned regularly could afford to be picky over such a trifle. An heiress was an heiress.

Lady Pomeroy had no more time to become better acquainted with Alyssa before the girl's first partner came to claim her. Even she knew when she was beaten, for all she said was, "I'll expect you tomorrow for tea, Pomeroy House, Portman Square." And with this peremptory invitation she reversed her majestic progress and returned to her chair among the matrons.

Alyssa enjoyed herself, despite her constant thoughts on the one subject that had brought her through these sacred portals. She accepted invitations to drive and ride, though the gentlemen involved were none she could easily picture herself marrying.

During a rest between dances, she sat with Aunt Henrietta and watched while Clara accepted yet another invitation to waltz with Sir Edward Talbot. She was speculating on the possibility that her stepmother might be falling in love, when a tall shadow fell across the floor in front of her.

She looked up, startled, to find Lord Brookmere bowing before her. He greeted Henrietta and asked how they were enjoying London, but looked only at her niece, and all the while Alyssa was incapable of uttering a word. She had not expected to see him back so soon, and certainly not at Almack's.

Henrietta, having earlier spotted Lord Robert Norton in the crowd, was bubbling with excitement. She simpered and plied her feather fan so vigorously that she tickled her nose and sneezed. "My Lord Brookmere! How lovely to see you again!"

To her raptures he replied almost as patiently as Sir Edward would have done, but before he could speak to Alyssa, Henrietta cried, "Dearest Alyssa is quite the belle of the evening, but I believe she has the next dance free." She glanced suggestively from one to the other.

Alyssa tried not to be annoyed at her aunt's well-meant interference, but she had no desire to dance with Lord Brookmere. Her debut at Almack's was not the time to become embroiled in an argument, as she always did when she was with him, and she would prefer not to make a spectacle of herself on the dance floor.

Her discomfort was soon to increase, for in the next moment Lord Robert approached Henrietta and bore her off for the quadrille, leaving her niece alone with the viscount.

To her relief, he did not ask her to dance. She had no idea that it was because he did not trust himself to be steady on his feet in his present condition. While not precisely foxed, he was a trifle disguised, and in any case was not in a dancing mood.

He had just returned from his visit to the Beddoes, a visit cut short by the fact that he had had no desire to fulfill the ambitions of the earl and his wife by asking for the hand of their daughter, Lady Jane, aged seventeen. Marriage, especially to a chit not yet out of the schoolroom, did not number among his lordship's plans. Indeed, he could not understand why they would wish to toss away their only child on a relatively pocket-pinched viscount. But one look at the thin, gawky young lady, with her plain face and unimproved mind showed him that her parents had more sense than he had given them credit for.

Not that it would have mattered if the young heiress had been of ethereal beauty, with a wit to equal it. Brookmere was determined not to bestow his hand on any lady till he could reasonably support her without the aid of her own fortune. His friends laughed at him, but he persevered in his contempt for the fortune seekers of his acquaintance, who flattered ugly heiresses and offered their titles in exchange for wealth.

With the exercise of the utmost tact, his lordship had managed to decline the honor of Lady Jane's hand without offending either the lady herself or her estimable parents. He returned to town, his honor and principles intact. It was not surprising, then, that such exertions would lead to an evening of overindulgence.

After a few pleasantly muddled hours at his club, he made his way to Almack's, just out of curiosity. A curiosity, he told himself, that had nothing to do with a certain young lady just arrived from the country, whom gossip said had squeaked by with the merest of luck in procuring vouchers.

"I congratulate you, Miss Wentworth. Here you are at Almack's, just as you once assured me you would be," he said, seating himself beside her. Alyssa bridled at his tone.

"Of course, my lord," she acknowledged coolly. She met his glance and wondered why it lacked the clarity she remembered.

"Ah, but how ungentlemanly of me to have doubted your word. And may I say that your beauty graces these rooms to perfection." His tone seemed sincere, but Alyssa doubted he really meant it. Besides, she wanted no compliments from this man.

There was something strange about Brookmere tonight, she thought, biting back a retort. For the first time, she saw no ridicule in his eyes. In spite of his quizzing attitude he looked tired, dispirited and, finally, as she caught the odor of brandy on his breath, rather drunk.

While she was not fond of the company of gentlemen in their cups, she recognized that he was troubled, and it could not help but disarm her.

"What is it, my lord?" she ventured at last. "Is there anything amiss?" She was immediately sorry, sure he would resent such presumption.

To her surprise he only smiled wearily. "You are perceptive, Miss Wentworth. Kind of you not to let your aunt press us into dancing. Perhaps you'll be kinder still and accompany me to an open window for some fresh air. It's damnably stuffy in here!"

With this he grasped her arm and Alyssa found herself being propelled through the rooms, all of which were crowded, until they came to one in which the only occupants were two young sprigs who stood grimacing over the scanty and uninteresting refreshments laid out on a table. At a glance from Brookmere, they abandoned their search for sustenance.

The viscount led Alyssa to an alcove, where he threw open a window and breathed deeply of the night air. It had happened so quickly, and she had not wanted to create a scene by refusing to accompany him. Now she was perilously aware of his closeness, and of the fact that someone might enter the room at any moment.

"Don't worry, my dear," he said, looking down at her frightened face, "I'm not an ogre, you know."

Alyssa relaxed a little and attempted to withdraw her arm, but he still held it in a firm grip.

"You are a sweet child to notice that I'm in a fit of the blue devils, but I'm afraid you will have to endure my dull company for a few minutes longer. I have no wish to return to that crush until I have had the benefit of some strong coffee," he said, scanning the table.

I must get control of this right now, Alyssa thought, her legs strangely weak as his fingers absently caressed her arm. She had no intention of allowing herself to be seen emerging from an alcove with Brookmere, whose every action remained the subject of gossip for weeks on end.

"I am not a child, my lord," she replied stiffly. "And I am certainly old enough to know when a gentleman has had more to drink than is good for him. I suggest you go home and have your valet put you to bed." She pulled away, but regretted her lack of tact, for suddenly he was pressing her against the wall, blocking her escape.

"Yes," he said softly, his glance slowly traveling the length of her body. "You are certainly no child. My apologies for not appearing to notice that before."

Alyssa could not find her voice, for her pounding heart seemed to press upward and block its escape as his burning gaze traced her curves.

Those deep blue eyes looked directly into hers and she could not look away. In a moment she was pressed against him and his arms held her tightly. It was altogether shocking and much too pleasant. A startled breath escaped her as she found her own arms twining about his neck.

When their lips met it was as if it were inevitable, and she was lifted on a wave of sensation even as he almost lifted her from the floor to meet his kiss. The touch of his mouth was tender and strange, unfamiliar feelings swept through her veins, leaving her with no desire to resist. For a long time Alyssa forgot where she was, even who she was, and everything seemed so right that she was lost to all shame.

When he finally set her down and released her she was only able to lean against him, her breath coming quickly, her mind in turmoil.

He looked down at her with a lazy smile and she almost returned it, when, with a start, she came back to earth. This was Almack's, where, if she were seen embracing a gentleman like a common wanton, her reputation would be in ruins and her chances of making the necessary marriage nil. For although this man might be the perfect answer to her dilemma, she had no illusions as to his feelings for her. Indeed, she would prefer a coldly negotiated business proposition than these terrifying caresses, full of passion but empty of feeling. For as she stood staring, speechless, she noticed how suddenly icy were his eyes.

"What is the matter, Miss Wentworth? Was it not...satisfactory?"

This was the final goad. Her emotions still raw and her body still trembling, Alyssa retorted, "I would not know what is satisfactory, my lord. You seem to have a false impression of my character, and you owe me an apology for taking advantage of me this way. You need not worry—I shall not cry out and you will not find yourself...encumbered. No one shall know of this episode from my lips."

Let him think what he wished. He was a man almost betrothed, according to all the gossip. She knew the kiss had meant nothing to him but a moment's stolen enjoyment and a test of her virtue. He would not have the opportunity to test it again, she vowed.

His brow was like a thundercloud. So the minx thought she could fool him, as if he were not man of the world enough to recognize the passion of a young lady's first kiss. Brookmere was not so foolish as to deny the very real attraction between them, but if she chose to deny it, he thought, it was her own affair.

"I beg your pardon, Miss Wentworth," he said, his voice hard, his face a study in disdain. "I did not realize that my attentions were so offensive. You shall not be troubled with them again."

"Please take me back to the ballroom," was all she could say, and he escorted her and left the assembly without addressing another word to her.

Neither of them had noticed the extravagantly dressed man who ducked back into the crowd as they emerged. Henry Basking smiled to himself, satisfied now with his night's work. By rights he ought to have been very alarmed by what he had witnessed. But instead he was hopeful, very hopeful, indeed.

CHAPTER EIGHT

THE SOUND OF HER MAID closing the door set Alyssa's temples to throbbing, and she winced as the curtains were parted and a shaft of sunlight fell across her pillow.

"Are you feeling poorly, miss? You're ever so pale." Nan's plain, red-cheeked face hovered over her, concerned.

"It is only the headache. Some strong coffee will set me right. And Nan, please tell Mrs. Wentworth and my aunt that I will not be coming down this morning."

When she was alone again she lay back against the pillows and held her hands up to her aching head. She had been relieved last evening to find that no one had noticed her prolonged absence. Clara had been too preoccupied and Henrietta too full of Lord Robert to spare a thought for her.

Alyssa had been in no spirits to enjoy the remainder of the evening, even the triumph of being at Almack's. Thankfully, before her smile grew too fixed, she was home in Green Street, where she finally fell into a restless sleep.

How would she ever face Lord Brookmere again? It was hardly likely that she could finish out the season without encountering him somewhere, and he was already engaged for their first dinner party, barely a week away.

Perhaps by then, she thought, she would have regained her composure, and in any case, there would be other guests to attend to. After that she ought to be far too busy to think of him, for the Wentworth ladies meant to begin entertaining in earnest.

Alyssa had every intention of remaining in bed for a good part of the day, until she recalled Lady Pomeroy's invitation. She wearily resigned herself to rising and joined the other two ladies in the sitting room, where they were compiling a guest list and menu for the dinner. Before the morning was far advanced Alyssa's headache was nearly gone, her appetite beginning to return after a prolonged discussion of delicacies.

It was shortly before luncheon when Oliver entered and announced a visitor. "Mr. Henry Basking," he intoned, his voice laden with disapproval.

All three ladies looked up in surprise. They had never expected him to present himself in Green Street after his sharp dismissal from Finchwood.

Mr. Basking, however, was not a bit perturbed as he swept into the room and performed an intricate bow. Today he was even more of a sight than before, sporting an "Oriental" neckcloth, a bright red-and-blue waistcoat beneath a coat of moss green and buff pantaloons. His collar was so high as to prevent him from turning his head.

Even Henrietta could find little to admire in this ambitious color scheme, and said as little as the other ladies in response to his florid greetings. After taking snuff in an elaborate ritual, Basking seated himself close to Alyssa.

"Dear ladies," he began, not looking at them but concentrating on replacing his large silver snuffbox in a tiny waistcoat pocket. "I noticed you made your debut at Almack's last evening, and was highly gratified that you, dear cousin, were received with the enthusiasm you deserve."

Henrietta was too proud of her niece's success to hold back. "It was delightful, Mr. Basking. Countess Lieven was so obliging, and all the gentlemen so charmed with dear Alyssa. Why, I believe she did not miss a single dance."

As if he had been awaiting a cue, Henry Basking smiled unpleasantly and remarked in knowing tones, "Surely there was one dance, Miss Wentworth, for which you did not appear. Nevertheless, I observed that you had a most attentive companion. I believe you were in search of some refreshment."

The unease that had haunted Alyssa since his arrival was now confirmed by these delicate hints. It was obvious that he had seen her alone with Brookmere. Panic welled up in her breast as she remembered how lost to everything she had been in his arms. If Basking had witnessed it, he would very likely use the information to discredit her. She must contrive to see him alone and find out just what he knew. Ignoring the looks of amazement on the faces of the other ladies, she accepted his invitation to drive in the park.

Alyssa was calm by the time she found herself in Henry Basking's curricle and she tried to analyze the situation coolly. It was possible that he had not seen the kiss, but only her withdrawal with Brookmere to the empty room. But whatever he had seen, he would be sure to ask a price for his silence, perhaps even the price of her hand in marriage.

As Basking guided his team toward the park, he also guided the conversation back to the subject of the night before.

"Such a squeeze as there was in those dismal rooms last night! You chose the perfect time to make your debut, my dear." He turned to her and smiled, but the look in his cold, pale gray eyes sent shivers of apprehension up Alyssa's spine.

"I must congratulate you on your conquest," he added casually.

Alyssa tried to laugh, but it was a poor, choked sound. "As to that, sir, several gentlemen were kind enough to ask me to stand up with them. It is a bit early to be speaking of conquests."

Not at all deterred, he continued smoothly, "My dear coz, your modesty is so becoming! But surely, and do not trouble to deny it, a very elevated person has found you...irresistible, and soon it will be on everyone's tongue that Lord Brookmere has found a new interest."

Alyssa was sure her voice would tremble and betray her, as she said, "Tell me, Mr. Basking, wherever did you get the idea that Lord Brookmere was so taken with me? I don't deny I sat out a dance with him, but—"

She had to stop, for they had entered the park and though it was not the fashionable hour for driving, several of her new acquaintances were out. She had just registered their surprise at seeing her with Henry Basking, when she had a surprise of her own to contend with. Coming toward them at a spanking pace was a gleaming black high-perch phaeton with yellow wheels, driven expertly by the Viscount Brookmere. Up beside him was a gorgeously attired woman, patently not a lady, her face obviously painted, her voice a little shrill as she laughed and clung to his arm.

His lordship, preoccupied with this female and his team of mettlesome chestnuts, did not see Alyssa until their carriages were almost at the point of passing. He only nodded to her briefly, his lips compressed and his eyes hooded, and bestowed a contemptuous glance upon her companion as they passed.

Alyssa had had time to do nothing but stare, wide eyed, at him, her heart in her throat and her face white. Yet it was only to be expected, she told herself, that such a man should parade his bits of muslin in the park after making love to a young lady in the ton's temple of respectability only the evening before.

She saw Basking's expression of sly satisfaction, and suddenly was too tired to continue the pretense.

"What is it that you want from me?" she asked coldly. "I know that you saw us...alone last night. Now just tell me how much you need not to speak to anyone of it, for I haven't the time or inclination to fence with you."

Basking could not hide his surprise and displeasure at her bluntness. "Of course I could expect nothing less from the daughter of a tradesman. Money, not honor, comes first to mind," he said with a sneer.

"It is useless to deny that you are in need of money, and as for honor, you would not be attempting to blackmail me if you had any use for it yourself," she answered disdainfully.

He reddened, but knowing that he held the winning hand, laid out his demand. "My one desire, sweet coz, is to be your own devoted husband and to join you in a life of wedded bliss at Finchwood. You must forgive my ill temper. I had the greatest respect for your papa—such an able fellow! Together you and I will enjoy the fruits of his labors."

Alyssa refused to be intimidated. She knew that the only thing he wanted out of the marriage was money, and money she could offer him. It would only be a temporary measure, but it would do for now. It might just be possible to explain away a large advance on the inheritance in a way that Mr. Noddley would not suspect.

She faced him without flinching and said in as confident a tone as she could manage, "You really don't wish to marry me. What you really want is my money, and you shall have it, as much of it as you need to pay your debts. Send me your bills, and I will pay them. But after that," she warned, "you'll get no more from me."

She saw his eyes widen and narrow again immediately, and his nostrils flared. "In return," she continued, encouraged, "you will engage to say nothing to anyone about what you thought you witnessed last night."

Alyssa could not know how timely her offer was, for it was only the day before that Henry Basking had returned to his Bond Street lodgings to find that the bailiff had been there, and had fled to the rooms of a friend to elude arrest. The present was too urgent. He would worry about the future, and the rest of the fortune, later.

"How very generous of you, Miss Wentworth," he replied. "You are correct in believing that I am not yet ready to settle to the connubial bond, despite the undeniable temptation of your charms."

Alyssa itched to slap the smirk from his face, but controlled herself by digging her nails into her palms.

"But there are a few, oh, very trifling sums owing to various tradesmen, and of course the debts of honor—so inconvenient!—that must be paid immediately. And I am sure you will agree that it would be wise and altogether desirable that I should refresh myself in the country for say, a month? The air of London," he said seriously, "is proving insalubrious to a gentleman of my constitution."

Alyssa was hard put not to collapse in relief. Very quickly it was all arranged and Basking turned his horse out of the park. As he helped Alyssa down before her door, he bowed over her hand. "It is a pleasure," he said unctuously, "to deal with a lady who conducts herself in such a businesslike way." At Alyssa's frown he added hastily, "And I give you my word as a gentleman that no word of detriment to your character shall pass my lips."

Reflecting silently that his word as a gentleman was undoubtedly useless but that she had no choice except to trust him, she left him without replying.

In the hall she found her aunt hopping about in agitation. "Oh, here you are at last! Clara would not leave until you returned, and we are expected at Lord Robert's to call upon his sister today. Do go in and see Clara, there's a good girl, and please tell her to hurry or we shall be late." Henrietta was so excited that the canary-yellow fringe on her blue jaconet muslin walking dress danced about her shoulders.

Alyssa was momentarily distracted from her troubles by the realization that she must now consider Lord Norton in the light of a possible uncle. She persuaded Henrietta to sit and sip a cordial, and hurried up to Clara, expecting a gentle interrogation.

Alyssa found it difficult to hide anything from her stepmother. Indeed, for a moment, she wished she could confide in her, but it would only make matters worse. She would simply have to convince Clara there was nothing amiss.

"I must own I was surprised, my dear, when you accepted Mr. Basking's invitation. After what he said—"

"But Clara, he is a relation, after all, and although I certainly don't care for him, I knew I should have to speak to him sometime or other," Alyssa replied glibly. "It seems that my greedy cousin noticed that not all the young men of the ton would scorn the daughter of William Wentworth and decided he ought to get his bid in before the auction was over."

Clara smiled, but persisted. "Whatever did he mean, though, by his remarks on your success at Almack's? There was something almost . . . ominous, in the way he—"

"Oh, you know that such a coxcomb cannot resist a bit of playacting." Alyssa shrugged this off scornfully. "He was just put out because my success last night weakens his chances of inheriting."

Her stepmother stared thoughtfully into space. "Well, it may be as you say . . ." She gathered her gloves and reticule. "I must go before poor Henrietta succumbs to a fit. Don't forget, my love, that you are to visit Lady Pomeroy.''

After changing into a green-sprigged muslin afternoon dress, with a wide flounced hem and a matching spencer trimmed in satin ruffles, Alyssa tied on a yellow satin bonnet, its broad bow perched fetchingly under the upturned brim. Accompanied by Nan, she set off for Portman Square.

As she relaxed her taut shoulders against the leather covered squabs of the carriage, Alyssa only hoped that she would not be too exhausted to give a good account of herself. She was sure that the old lady would have no patience with anyone not as vigorous and clearheaded as herself.

Pomeroy House was grand and imposing, and Alyssa felt a chill as she was ushered through the echoing public rooms that looked too elegant for comfort. Thus she was pleasantly surprised when she was at length shown into a jewel of a sitting room with rugs and draperies of warm red.

Here she found her great-aunt enthroned in a satin armchair, her surprisingly small feet resting on a matching footstool. Lady Pomeroy wore a gown of brown sarsenet, modestly trimmed with little jewelry. Her appearance was in marked contrast to the night before, when she had been swathed in puce silk and hung with the Pomeroy diamonds.

She gestured peremptorily to Alyssa. "Well, come along there, gel. Come right up where I can get a good look at you in daylight." She raised a quizzing glass, peered at Alyssa and, seemingly satisfied, motioned for her to sit down. "Yes, you're a pretty thing— healthy enough, too, by the look of you. You'll want some food." She reached for a bell that sat on the table next to her, and a footman and parlormaid entered almost immediately with trays of tea, bread and butter, cakes and sweetmeats. Lady Elizabeth looked on approvingly as Alyssa poured the tea at her request.

"Graceful, and very pretty mannered, no doubt. Well, I'm convinced. Happy to say that your grandparents were even more foolish than I thought them twenty years ago."

She lifted a Sevres teacup to her lips, sipped and set it down. "Your papa may have been a merchant, but there's not a sign of it in you." She ate a sweetmeat with some satisfaction.

"My father," said Alyssa with quiet dignity, "was a gentlemanly, cultured man. He read a great deal and appreciated music and beautiful things. He was a good husband and a loving parent, and I consider the fact that he had a talent for business to be to his credit rather than a disadvantage."

Surprisingly, the old lady apologized. "Sorry, child, no need to fly up into the boughs. In my day his kind were no more cultured than my stableboy. I have eyes. I can tell you've been properly brought up. Of course, your mama was a Sydney, and the second wife is a ladylike little thing, as well. I'd like to have known your papa. Must have been quite a man to have had two such women marry him."

Alyssa was mollified, and realized that she had to make allowances for an old woman who was accustomed to speaking her mind.

"But your aunt," continued Lady Pomeroy indignantly. "Never have I seen such a bird-witted female!

That gown! How did you let her leave the house in such a getup!''

Alyssa tried not to smile.

"Heard a rumor that Norton might actually offer for her." Lady Pomeroy added, before Alyssa could answer. "All I can say is he must be a bigger mutton-head than I'd taken him for. If I know that dried up old stick of a sister of his, she'll see that nothing comes of it. Best warn that silly aunt of yours, gel. Wouldn't do for her to be disappointed.''

Alyssa protested that matters had not yet progressed that far, but Lady Pomeroy interrupted with a wave of her hand that sent the crumbs of her cake scattering into a corner, where a fat pug lazily waddled over to investigate them.

"Don't tell me, child. Nothing wrong with my ears, at least. I hear everything that goes on in town, and sometimes I don't leave the house for a fortnight. Do you understand?''

Alyssa said that she did, and wondered what else her ladyship had heard lately. Her curiosity was not long in being satisfied, for Lady Elizabeth began on the subject of Henry Basking.

"Toad-eating fop. Can't wonder at it. His mother was enough to sour milk—don't dare show her face anymore. The whole family's been in Queer Street ever since the old baronet took to playing macao and keeping opera dancers and the like—very expensive, those birds of paradise. Why, I recall the days when my Henry—'' She broke off abruptly remembering the tender age of her audience. "Hmmph. Never you mind that, gel. Gerald Basking was an old fool and the grandson's like a muling, whey-faced girl. Heard you were driving with him this morning, miss. Now what's that all about?'' she demanded, placing her empty cup on an enameled tray.

Alyssa's head was whirling with the swift change of subjects. At first she tried to be noncommittal about her drive with her cousin, but Lady Pomeroy was not to be put off so easily.

''Don't want to talk about it, eh? Well, then, I'll talk. Saw that knock-in-the-cradle Basking last night at Almack's watching you with that handsome viscount—what's his name?''

''Brookmere,'' said Alyssa, looking down at her hands, knotted in her muslin lap.

''Brookmere, yes. Ah, now there's a man!'' The old lady sighed gustily. ''Wouldn't mind being twenty— no, make that thirty—years younger.'' She glanced sharply at Alyssa, who made no response.

''Basking was standing in the doorway of an empty room, lurking like the cat before the mousehole, staring at nothing *I* could see.''

Alyssa could not look up.

''Then he scurried away, and out came you and that Brookmere fellow. Now, miss, have you any idea what might've made Basking act like that?''

''I—I don't know, Aunt Elizabeth.'' Alyssa was totally occupied now in rolling and unrolling the fingers of her gloves.

''Stop that, gel. You're ruining 'em. If you want something to do with your hands I'll let you work on my netting.''

Alyssa sighed, put aside the gloves and finally looked up. Her great-aunt was still watching her closely. The old lady said, in surprisingly kind tones,

"Come on, then, let's have the whole story out. I can see you ain't the carefree miss I first met last night."

To her horror, Alyssa found herself bursting into tears.

CHAPTER NINE

ALYSSA BLEW HER NOSE again on one of Lady Pomeroy's fine lawn handkerchiefs. Before she knew what she was about, she found herself telling the entire story, from the shock of her father's will to the narrowly averted disaster that morning, while her great-aunt listened in silence. Lady Elizabeth let her cry and talk, told her to blow her nose and dry her eyes as if she had been a child, and poured her another cup of tea.

"Well, you've got a head on your shoulders, at least. There's many a female would've come to grief in such a situation long before this. Too bad about the money, though—a demmed waste, as Basking will be on tick again before year's end. As for that young buck, your viscount, well obviously he's your man. He's titled, well born and a handsome devil. And though you won't admit it, you're in love with him," she said matter-of-factly.

Alyssa's eyebrows flew up. "I am most certainly not! He is the most odious beast imaginable. Just because he kissed me does not mean that he wants to marry me. Or that I want to marry him," she added.

Lady Pomeroy laughed. "You may deny it child, but I've lived a sight longer than you and I've seen it happen many times. Besides, Basking wasn't the only one watching you two last night. Brookmere may have been a trifle bosky, but it only helped him get his courage up, in my opinion. He's probably been wanting to kiss you since the day you met." She chuckled. "And whether you admit it or not, if he offered for you, you'd have him."

"No!" cried Alyssa. "I am no more to him than that female he was driving with in the park today. I'm just someone he amuses himself with. I wouldn't marry such a man if he were my last chance."

"Have it your own way, then, miss," Lady Elizabeth said, temporarily conceding defeat. "At least Basking will be out of your hair for the time being. But don't think he won't be back with a new demand," she warned. "As I see it, you've got a clear month to get all this settled. Now that list of yours, the one that solicitor drew up for you, who else is on it?"

Alyssa gave the names, embarrassed now that she had ever thought such a scheme could work.

"Well, Norton's out of it, but he wouldn't have done for you, anyway. What was the fellow thinking of? The Talbot fellow's well enough, but I hear he has eyes for no one but your stepmama. Hmm, Lord Lynwood, no, he's a squint-eyed fellow, no experience with women, either."

She sat back, wrinkling her already lined forehead as she tried to recall all the gossip she'd heard in the past thirty years. "Selbridge, yes, he might just do," she mused. "Not as handsome as some, but pleasant and quick-witted. Yes, I shall introduce you. Come to dinner Saturday. He'll be there."

Alyssa smiled through her tears at her great-aunt's certainty that she could produce earls at her dinner table at will.

Lady Elizabeth noticed her amusement. "And why not? Known him since he was in short coats—known all of them, in fact, and like as not their parents and their grandparents, too. And of course they all know me. I tell you he'll be there. Now Mannerly," she continued, "there's a splendid catch for a girl. The duke's a miserable old cheeseparer, but he'll be winding up his accounts soon enough. Liver trouble," she added by way of explanation. "The son's good-looking, not too much in the attic, but you've got more than enough for both of you. He'll be there, too, and you can see if you like either of them."

This time Alyssa did not laugh. She was beginning to believe that if the prince regent himself were summoned to Pomeroy House, he would obey instantly.

"Then it will be you, your stepmother and even that prattle-box aunt of yours, and I'll invite Norton to keep her from annoying us. Talbot, of course, and his sisters. Mannerly, Selbridge, and—oh, some others. And now you may leave," she said, abruptly rising and reaching for an ivory cane. "I'm tired and it's time for my rest."

She brushed off Alyssa's thanks and apologies for behaving like such a watering pot. "No need to thank me, my dear. Just come Saturday and wear a pretty gown, and within a month we'll see you settled."

Alyssa, once she was back home, could not believe that the events of the afternoon had really happened. It was an enormous relief to be able to confide in someone who seemed to know all the answers to her problems. She only hoped she could find something to like in the two gentlemen who would be presented to her on Saturday, but was strangely apathetic.

Recalling her great-aunt's comments, she forced herself to face the possibility that she might really be in love with Viscount Brookmere. But when she envisioned his frigid countenance and uncompromising figure, all she felt was a cold shrinking feeling deep in her chest.

She remembered all too clearly the mutual antipathy in which they had last parted company. No, she decided with great relief, it could not possibly be true. Her warm response to his kiss could not easily be explained, but he was, after all, an attractive man, with a certain charm when it pleased him to exert it. Perhaps it was only that he had caught her by surprise.

SATURDAY ARRIVED, and Alyssa was beginning to feel like herself again. No more was heard from Basking after his bills were paid and she assumed he had gone to the country. She had been forced to draw an advance of a month's worth of income and to use all the cash at her disposal in order to pay them, and only hoped that Mr. Noddley could be fobbed off and kept unaware of the use to which such a sum had been put.

She was not surprised when Oliver announced the solicitor that morning. However, Noddley's extreme agitation told her at once that he had not come to discuss her spendthrift behavior. He would not sit down, but would only pace back and forth, wringing his hands.

"Miss Wentworth, I am so sorry, so terribly sorry," he said, distraught. "Of course when I discover the villain responsible he shall be turned off without a character immediately! My own desk! To think that this should happen—a matter so very confidential!"

He seemed not to realize that he was making no sense, so Alyssa spoke softly to him, made him sit down and gave him a glass of brandy. When he was somewhat calmer, she asked, "My dear Mr. Noddley, whatever has occurred to distress you so?"

"The list," he said after a swallow of brandy, "it is gone." He put down his glass with a trembling hand.

At first she was bewildered, but then her hands grew cold and her legs weak and she took a seat beside him.

"Tell me," she said from between lips frozen with fear.

"I left my offices yesterday afternoon about half-past five, but two streets away I recalled that there were some papers I had meant to bring home with me. I went back—and found my desk in disorder, the drawers pulled out, files opened and scattered everywhere and your own personal file open on top of the desk. It was obvious that several things were missing. One of them—" he gulped and took her hand "—was the list of eligible gentlemen I made up at your request."

He saw her turn white and hastily poured a glass of brandy for her, which she sipped until the room steadied about her and some color returned to her cheeks.

"Oh, Mr. Noddley," she whispered chokingly. "To think what could happen if that list were seen by anyone—especially the gentlemen concerned. Why, we would be made either a scandal or a laughingstock, and I can't say I know which would be worse. No one who knew of it would wish to have anything to do with me, and as for my plans..."

She closed her eyes, took a long breath and tried not to give in to hysteria. "We must discover who took it and get it back, or at the very least prevent them from using the information to harm my reputation."

"Indeed, Miss Wentworth, it is very likely that it is already too late. However can we find the culprit? No one in my offices saw anyone enter or leave the room, but the window opening on an alley was ajar—it was plain that whoever it was observed me till I left, then took the opportunity to make the search and escape through the window."

A chilling thought had occurred to Alyssa. "Do you recall, Mr. Noddley, our surprise at the fact that my cousin Basking should know in advance about the contents of Papa's will?" she asked.

"I remember it quite well, especially as I was afraid that I had been derelict in my duties, since I myself should have been the one to inform him, but I could not bear to tell him before you learned of it. But what has that got to do with—"

"I am very much afraid, Mr. Noddley, that since my cousin is the only likely person who would have any interest in the contents of the file or the list, that he himself, or perhaps a hired spy, has made off with it."

"By God, it cannot be! That any nephew of William could stoop to such—"

"But how else," Alyssa persisted, "would he have found out about the contents of the will, unless he had already, in secret, seen it in your office? I assure you, I have no confidence at all in my cousin's character. I

am willing to believe that he would stoop to anything
to take Finchwood from me."

Noddley shook his head. "I don't know what we
can do, except confront him and try to recover the
papers. Perhaps if I offered him a sum of money—"

"You will do no such thing!" cried Alyssa, horrified at the shabby trick her cousin had played her,
though she had paid his debts. "Besides," she added
a little more calmly, "I have heard that he is gone away
to the country for a few weeks. Surely he can do me no
harm while he is not in town to spread his vicious re-
ports. In any case, I will not stand by while a penny of
my money—or yours, either—goes into that scoun-
drel's pockets. You must promise me that you will do
nothing for now."

The solicitor, after a little argument, reluctantly
promised to wait upon events. "I've been a poor
counselor to you, my dear, and your papa would have
had me skinned alive for an episode like this. I should
never have permitted you to talk me into it."

"No, my dear Noddley, it is entirely my fault, for
being so stubborn as to insist on that silly plan. You
would never had made up that list if I had not plagued
you to death over it. You, at least, shall have a clear
conscience." She tried to smile. "Don't worry, we shall
come about."

At length he departed, leaving her to brood over her
foolishness and what it had brought her to. No doubt
her cousin would have to be silenced with more
money. If only she could keep him from insisting on
marrying her. It was a grim thought, but if he spread
his scandals, he could leave her with no choice for a
husband but himself.

The Wentworth ladies spent the rest of the day quietly, and Alyssa did not reveal her anxiety either to her aunt or her stepmother. Neither of them was interested in Noddley's visit, Clara going about distracted with a smile on her lips and Henrietta in despair.

It seemed that the visit to Lord Robert Norton's sister had been a dismal failure. That lady, who had kept her brother's home and been his hostess for the past ten years, was jealous of any interference and afraid of having her place usurped by a sister-in-law. She had driven off many ladies hopeful of becoming Lady Norton, and her brother mildly submitted to her tyranny.

"She was as cold as ice to us, my love," complained Henrietta to her niece, "and she was so rude as to say that she positively loathed pleated sarsenet and that she hoped never again to see the color fuchsia on a lady past five-and-twenty!"

Alyssa murmured her sympathy, but secretly agreed with the unknown Miss Norton.

"Well, she soon learned to mend her manners after I looked about the room as though it were the merest rustic cottage and asked if it was her little goddaughter who had embroidered the firescreens for her." Henrietta's round face beamed with satisfaction. "Poor Robert was so shocked, for he himself had told me that she had spent quite six months working on them and that I must be sure to praise them excessively."

Alyssa could not hold back her laughter. "My dear aunt, I vow I am beginning to pity poor Miss Norton! However can you expect to get along comfortably with her if you return her rudeness in kind? You must instead try to win her over."

"I was perfectly ready to be her friend, but she took against me before she even met me. She is jealous of my influence over her brother. She fears to lose her place if Lord Robert and I were to—"

"Aunt Henrietta, has he made you an offer? Am I to wish you happy?"

A tear found its way down Henrietta's plump cheek. "No, not yet, and after the visit with his sister, we had words...." She sniffled and searched in her reticule for a handkerchief. "We are no longer speaking. I warned him that she was trying to separate us, that he would lose my friendship as he has lost that of other ladies and that it was all his fault for letting his sister frighten them away."

She sniffed loudly and wiped at the stream of tears. "He was horrid to me! I told him that I would not see him again until he was ready to apologize. And—and I told him he need not come to our dinner party next week, even if we do have uneven numbers!"

Alyssa tried to comfort her. "There now, Aunt, it's only a lovers' quarrel. He'll soon see reason, and his sister will have to realize that she can't stop him from marrying if he is really determined to do so. Besides," she added, knowing that her aunt could be easily distracted from tears to joy, "he is to be at Lady Pomeroy's tonight. She said she was inviting him especially for you." Alyssa forgave herself this little tampering with the truth. "Why don't you try to look as pretty as you can? When he sees you he will beg your forgiveness and you can go on as before."

Henrietta stopped crying. "What a wonderful idea. I shall dazzle him with my elegance. Shall it be the cherry satin? Or the emerald crepe with the jonquil underskirt?" She wandered away to plan the evening's toilette.

When the ladies descended to the hall to wait for their carriage that evening, it was Alyssa's costume that drew the most attention, though Henrietta, in a fit of uncertainty, had decked herself in almost every color of the rainbow.

"You are in splendid looks tonight, my love," said Clara. "That lovely coral is so becoming."

"I agree," Henrietta chimed in, "though I wish you would not feel the need to confine yourself to only *one* color in your costume, Alyssa."

"But the darker shade of rosebuds scattered over the skirt gives it a contrast and prevents it from looking too demure," Clara interceded.

The gown was far from demure, Alyssa felt, and not because of the rosebuds. The neckline, in fact, was much lower than she was accustomed to wearing, but the modiste had assured her of its perfect propriety. The coral shade gave a creamy tint to her curving bosom, elegant shoulders and neck adorned only with a single strand of perfect pearls. Despite being a bit uncomfortable at exposing so much, Alyssa was sure that Lady Pomeroy would approve.

Clara and Henrietta were awed by the richness of Pomeroy House and even Alyssa was excited as they drew up to the torchlit entrance. This night, she knew, would be crucial to her plans.

Lady Pomeroy, elegant in silver-gray satin, stood leaning on an ebony cane in the entrance of the large drawing room. She welcomed the Wentworth ladies and waved them majestically into the room, regarding Clara and Alyssa with approval. When she saw the nervously smiling and brightly attired Henrietta she shut her eyes for a moment.

As that extravagantly gowned lady hurried across the room to where a gloomy Lord Robert stood in ill-fitting evening clothes and while Clara was being spirited away by an eager Sir Edward, Lady Elizabeth took her great-niece aside.

"Had the devil of a time getting Norton here," she said irritably. "Seems they've quarreled. I hope they settle it before dinner. Melodrama interferes with my digestion."

But Alyssa barely heard her. At the far end of the room stood a familiar tall figure, and at the sight of him her heart pounded against her coral silk bodice and blood roared in her ears. She was unconsciously backing away, when she felt Lady Pomeroy's hand on her arm.

"Don't be such a widgeon, gel. The man don't bite. He's half in love with you already, even if you can't see it. Besides—" she gave a dry chuckle "—have to speak to him sometime. You're sitting next to him at dinner."

CHAPTER TEN

BROOKMERE STOOD with Sir Edward and Clara and the two Miss Talbots. He glanced up and saw Alyssa's large, frightened eyes on him, but she looked away before he could acknowledge her presence.

Trying to still her unreasonable fear, she pushed aside the burning memory of the kiss she had failed to resist and told herself that this was no reason for the evening to be ruined. *I shall always be meeting him somewhere,* she thought, *and I shall just have to become accustomed to talking to him as if he were simply another acquaintance.* It would only be food for gossip if they ignored each other.

This thought steadied her nerves and she advanced into the room. She saw her Aunt Henrietta beckoning to her, and relieved that she could still postpone the meeting with Brookmere, she joined the now reconciled couple. Henrietta was simpering and giggling like any girl with her first beau, and Lord Robert, a thin smile lighting his bleak countenance, seemed equally happy with his overdressed inamorata.

"My dear, whatever do you think? Lord Norton has had a serious talk with his sister, and he has convinced her, as I knew he could do, not to interfere in our . . . friendship."

She smiled proudly at her swain. "We are quite in charity with each other again, and Miss Norton even said that she would like to call on me that we may begin again and learn to be friends."

Alyssa congratulated them on solving their difficulty so happily. How she wished that her own situation could be handled so simply. Yet why could it not? If a nervous, jealous spinster like Miss Norton responded to a little plain speaking, would an elegant, though hot-blooded lord take it amiss if she simply spoke a few sensible words to him? It just might work, she thought.

Lady Pomeroy at that moment approached her in company with two unknown gentlemen. "Selbridge, Mannerly, this is Miss Alyssa Wentworth, my niece Elizabeth's girl."

The old lady looked keenly from one to the other as if to spy out the first hint of an attraction.

Selbridge, the earl, was a stocky man of medium height, with the ruddy complexion of the sportsman and thick, curling brown hair. He was not unattractive and he bowed very gracefully over Alyssa's hand, glancing up at her with merry brown eyes.

"A pleasure to make your acquaintance, Miss Wentworth." He eyed her with slightly more than friendly interest. "I hear that it is only lately that you come to be known to her ladyship," he said, looking fondly at Lady Elizabeth. "It is a pity that you missed the benefits of her, er...guidance during your childhood. She will ever remain a major figure in the memory of my own early years," he added, one hand straying waggishly to the seat of his breeches, as if that memory still pained him.

Lady Pomeroy let forth with a guffaw and made as if to rap his knuckles with her fan. "Well, sir, it was your own fault for thinking that you could run wild through my roses while your mama visited me. To my mind you didn't get half as many canings as you deserved in those days."

Lord Mannerly, though not so cheerful, had a charming smile. He was, in fact, an Adonis of a man, tall, fair, well built, but with a vapidity of expression and a dullness to his conversation that made him lose half his attractiveness in Alyssa's eyes.

"Have you been very long in town, Miss Wentworth?" he inquired, his pale blue eyes serious.

"Hardly a month, my lord," she replied, "but I am enjoying it after living in the country."

"Whereabouts is your home?"

"A day's drive from Canterbury, sir, a pleasant little town called Swinbury. Perhaps you have heard of it?"

His lordship regretted that he had not.

And so on, until Alyssa began to chafe under the tedium of such commonplaces.

Fortunately the earl soon claimed her attention again, and she found him much more to her taste. He complimented her without overdone flattery; he made clever jests and was charmingly attentive to her great-aunt. Alyssa was soon so relaxed in his company that even the approach of Lord Brookmere with Clara and the Talbots failed to throw her into the panic she had anticipated.

She remained outwardly calm as she presented the earl and Lord Mannerly to Clara, but she was intensely aware of a pair of deep blue eyes regarding her all the while. Her mouth felt dry and her palms damp, and she found it hard to keep from meeting the viscount's gaze. She only felt safe when, the introductions made, she risked a quick glance and found that his face held no more than an expression of polite interest.

Neither of the two Talbot sisters was acquainted with Selbridge, and any qualms they may have had about the advisability of associating with the Wentworths were banished at once by this opportunity. The elder Miss Talbot blushed charmingly when he addressed her, while Miss Julia Talbot soon gave her attention to Lord Mannerly and hung on his every word as if he were a wit of the first order.

Alyssa observed all this with a sad smile. Why did it seem as though every man on her horrid list was destined for another woman? All except one, apparently, for Henrietta had informed her only the other day that the rumors of Lord Brookmere's engagement had faded away.

Now, she thought as she saw his lordship looking at her with unguarded appreciation, now was her chance to set things right, to embark on a course of normalcy and give up the turbulence of their past association. As for the kiss, she must pretend it had never happened.

She gathered her courage and forced herself to approach Brookmere, fixing her earnest green gaze on his face.

"My lord, my great-aunt informs me that we are seated together at dinner. I am aware that in the past we have not . . . that is, we began our acquaintance in an unfortunate manner, and since then..." Alyssa paused and felt the heat of a blush rising to her cheeks.

She looked away and felt him move closer. His nearness had an unfortunate effect on her voice and she spoke quickly, as if afraid she would be unable to finish before it disappeared completely.

"I have made up my mind that, although perhaps we were not precisely meant to be friends, we can at least be civil to each other and I will try not to provoke you if you will give me your promise to do the same," she finished in a rush, hating her own timidity.

"And the events of our last meeting—excuse me, our last meeting in private?" His voice was cool and amused.

His indifference gave her courage. "We will pretend, sir," she said forcing herself to meet his gaze, "that it did not occur."

"Ah, but did you think I could forget so easily," he said softly.

"My lord, if you think for one moment—" Anger at her failure strengthened her voice and made her eyes flash.

"Forgive me, Miss Wentworth, but I could not resist teasing you." His smile was one of pure enjoyment. "I offer my apologies for the mistakes of the past, and I will accept your little speech as an apology of your own. No, do not get on your high ropes, for you know that we are equally at fault. From this moment," he said, placing her hand on his arm, for the guests were now being summoned to dinner, "we shall be new acquaintances, and the past is forgotten."

As he led her into the dining room, Alyssa felt weak from relief. Her idea had obviously had the desired effect.

Some twenty people sat down in the blue-and-gold room with its polished floor, in which the lights from the silver candelabra were reflected. Her ladyship's French chef had prepared a repast fit for a far more formal occasion, but her ladyship had never believed in stinting where food was concerned. Clear soup and poached salmon with dill sauce were followed by braised sweetbreads, a shoulder of lamb, roasted capon, two removes of vegetables, a fine joint of beef and an endless procession of side dishes, till Alyssa wondered how she would find time to address even a word to the viscount between bites.

They were seated opposite Clara and Sir Edward, who were totally absorbed in each other, much to the amusement of Lady Pomeroy and her contemporaries, who winked and nodded at this evidence of a probable forthcoming match. On Alyssa's left was Lord Mannerly, but after a few exchanges about the food, the company to be found in town and the entertainments they had so far attended, he allowed his attention to be monopolized by Julia Talbot, and Alyssa was left to Lord Brookmere.

She was pleasantly surprised, for he did indeed behave as if they were newly introduced, and questioned her about her life in Swinbury. Indeed, he seemed so interested in the village he had once scorned that she began to wonder if he were not a completely different person from the man who had so precipitately taken her into his arms.

This new Brookmere was intelligent, amusing and flatteringly attentive. He drew her out so much that she finally stopped, embarrassed, for she had hardly given him a chance to say anything.

"My lord, you have let me run on in the most shameful way," she said, shaking her head at a footman who offered her more wine. Though she had drunk little, it had already gone to her head. "I am sure I must have bored you long before now, yet you have been too kind to say so. It is only fair that I should stop and give you a chance."

He swirled the ruby liquid in his glass and laughed. "What, are you giving *me* a chance to bore *you*?"

She smiled, but would not talk again of herself. "Tell me about your home. Where is it?"

"Brookmere is half a day's drive from London in good weather and with my fastest grays poled up to my best curricle," he replied with a twinkle in his eye. "It's not far from Cambridge. We have been in possession of the land since Tudor times." He went on to describe the manor, the gallery where the portraits of his ancestors hung and, with infectious enthusiasm, his well-stocked stables and all the improvements he had made to the property, his face glowing with pride.

Alyssa had never imagined such a side to him, and was amazed to find herself discussing such things as improvements to tenants' cottages, new farming methods and above all horses, which were his passion. She had gained her knowledge of these matters from many talks with her father and had not expected to be able to use any of it in conversation with a noted Corinthian.

Brookmere, in his turn, was impressed by Alyssa's proficiency in these interesting subjects, which hardly a single young lady of the ton could even approach. Without thinking he said, "Brookmere is delightful in midsummer, when my mother's garden is in full bloom. Perhaps you will see it one day."

At this a curious shyness overcame her and she hastily gave her attention to a recalcitrant pile of minted peas, which huddled at the edge of her plate and refused to climb aboard her fork.

Fortunately, before his lordship could either think better of his impromptu invitation or press it further, a footman removing plates between courses forced a pause in their talk. Distracted from Alyssa by his other neighbor, Brookmere turned away with obvious reluctance.

Alyssa listened to the murmur of conversation and tried to reconcile her new impressions of Lord Brookmere with all her former knowledge of him. She watched him, noting his determined gestures, his sudden smiles and his habit of impatiently shaking back a falling wave of brown hair when he leaned forward to emphasize a point.

She turned away to see her stepmother watching her curiously from across the table. Hurriedly she began to address her plate of strawberries Chantilly, savoring the tart fruit and letting the cream melt on her tongue as she tried to make some order out of her muddled emotions.

"Forgive me, Miss Wentworth, if I appear to have been neglecting you." The viscount's deep rich voice broke into her thoughts, and his smile as he turned to her was completely and utterly disarming.

"No, not at all, my lord," she said quickly. She had the curious feeling that he knew she had been thinking about him.

"Of what were we speaking?"

"I—I can't seem to recall."

"Nor can I."

They could not look away from each other. His gaze was curious, seeking, and hers cautious, almost unbelieving. Alyssa was suddenly grateful for the support of the chair beneath her, but in a moment she was to be deprived of it, for Lady Pomeroy had stood, a signal to the ladies to withdraw. Her ladyship had been watching the couple with satisfaction, and had lingered at the table as long as possible for their benefit, but it was far past time for the ladies to retire.

"Very well, gentlemen, we will leave you to your port. Never could stand the stuff myself, but the late Baron insisted, and I suppose you will want it. Don't keep us waiting too long."

With an uncertain smile for Brookmere, Alyssa rose and followed the other ladies back to the drawing room, relieved at the prospect of a brief respite from the increasing intimacy of their conversation.

The viscount gazed after her trim figure, wondering if this charming, intelligent female was the same girl who had once approached him in such a forward and vulgar manner. Her sudden change of manner puzzled him and for a moment he wondered if there could be an ulterior motive to her actions. He brooded until called to attention by the bottle being passed along the table.

While the ladies awaited coffee and the return of the gentlemen, their drawing room conversation centered on a recent, scandalous elopement by the daughter of an earl with an enterprising half-pay officer. While Lady Pomeroy and her cronies railed against such a crime, Henrietta defended the lovers in an impassioned way that made the baroness groan and reach for a pastille to soothe her digestion.

"How dreadful it must have been for them, the poor dears! To be forbidden to marry is so shocking. A family should never interfere in the course of true love!"

Some of the company, recalling the circumstances of the Wentworths' marriage, began to look uncomfortable. Swiftly, Lady Elizabeth stepped in and changed the subject, shooting a dark look at Henrietta. The latter was not at all discouraged, and talked on at length to anyone who would listen about her ideas on true love. Lady Pomeroy merely grunted and looked at Alyssa as if to say, "What is the use?"

Happily, the gentlemen were not long in joining them and Henrietta was distracted from her monologue by the entrance of Lord Robert.

Averting her eyes from the scene of their tender reunion, Lady Pomeroy looked on approvingly as the Viscount Brookmere chose a seat next to her greatniece. She congratulated herself on her cleverness and the subtlety with which she had placed that dull dog, Lord Mannerly, at Alyssa's other side.

Now she only hoped that the stubborn chit would keep her temper and not cause Brookmere to lose his. If all went well, she would see them married by the end of the year or earlier. Brookmere, she knew, was not a patient man.

Anxiety crept over Alyssa as the sofa cushion sank under Brookmere's weight. Suddenly the vast room seemed tiny and the sofa much too small. He seemed to radiate a warmth and excitement that confused her senses, and she hardly knew how to reply when he said abruptly, "The evening is half over, Miss Wentworth, and you have not yet told me when I will see you again."

"Why, you are invited to dinner next Tuesday, my lord, and have been for weeks, ever since you came to visit us at Finchwood," she finally managed.

His smile made her heart flutter. "So I have, and I remember the occasion well, but according to our agreement I mustn't speak of it," he teased. "However, this will not do at all. Tuesday is much too faraway. Come drive with me in the park tomorrow."

Alyssa's smile was as bright as his. "I—I would like that very much."

Their conversation was interrupted at this point by Miss Munsen, Lady Pomeroy's companion, who came to ask if they would care to make up a table for whist. Alyssa did not care for cards, and Brookmere, usually an avid player, had no intention of being chained to a card table when there were so many interesting possibilities to explore.

"No, thank you, Miss Munsen, but I have another form of entertainment in mind. Would you be so kind as to ask Lady Pomeroy if we may open the pianoforte? I have no doubt that the young ladies will oblige us with some music."

The spare gray Miss Munsen blushed like a schoolgirl under the influence of his smile and hurried away to relay the message.

Her ladyship glanced up from her cards. "Of course, Brookmere, an excellent idea. You young people enjoy yourselves."

All who were not at cards gathered around the instrument and one by one the ladies declined the honor of playing first, until it was decided that Julia Talbot would begin. Alyssa was relieved, for though she loved music she had not practiced much of late.

James Carstairs engaged Brookmere in conversation, and Mary, looking radiant but not yet obviously enceinte, took a chair next to Alyssa and complimented her on her looks.

"London certainly agrees with you, my dear." She drew closer and whispered, "And when am I to wish you happy?" Her eyes went to Lord Brookmere.

Alyssa knew that she was turning pink and protested that Mary was jumping to conclusions.

"Don't trouble to deny it, you slyboots." Mary smiled at her friend's embarrassment. "The way he looks at you—"

"Mary, please do not be starting rumors. It is nothing at all. Why, we barely know each other. It is ridiculous to be talking of it so soon."

Mary apologized and the subject was dropped, but Alyssa worried lest Brookmere had overheard them. Then he would think she was on the catch for him, and would no doubt be as disgusted with her as when they had first met. And, at this moment she wanted nothing to mar the new harmony she had found in his company.

CHAPTER ELEVEN

A STILL SLEEPY Lord Brookmere was just shrugging into his dressing gown, when his valet informed him that a Mr. Henry Basking was waiting in the library to speak to him.

"Who the devil is he?" grumbled his lordship.

"I am sure I do not know, my lord," replied Mallow, managing to convey the impression that the visitor was not the sort of person he thought a fit acquaintance for his employer. "The gentleman says that he must see you on a matter of some importance, and it is urgent, as he is leaving for the country immediately. He regrets the necessity of having to disturb you so early."

"Well, if he is in such a blasted hurry, he'll just have to speak to me while I have my breakfast. Damned impertinence," he muttered while Mallow put his sleep-tousled hair into some semblance of order.

"Have a tray sent to me in the library."

Though irritated at the intrusion of this unknown Mr. Basking, the viscount was far calmer than he would have been had he not just spent one of the most pleasant evenings of his life. The beautiful Miss Wentworth had surprised him by suing for peace, and for his part he had been happy enough to call a truce. Thus when his lordship saw what awaited him in the library, he was shaken rudely out of his pleasant mood and the tune he was whistling died on his lips.

Mr. Basking was resplendent in skintight pantaloons, and a wasp-waisted, double-breasted coat. His dress failed to impress Lord Brookmere, who watched contemptuously as his guest minced toward him.

"My Lord Brookmere, please forgive my intruding upon you at such a heathenish hour. I assure you I would never have dared disturb you if I were not just on the point of leaving town. I simply had to speak to you before leaving for Dunscombe."

The viscount waved away these apologies with an impatient hand. "Never mind all that. State your business, man, and let me get on with my breakfast." A footman had entered bearing a huge tray covered with plates of eggs, bacon, fresh bread with butter and jam, a large, rare chop and a pot of coffee. "Can I offer you anything?"

Mr. Basking paled at the sight of so much food. He was not accustomed to putting anything solid into his stomach until well past noon. "No, thank you, my lord. Indeed, I feel a bit queasy."

The viscount shrugged and set to work with a hearty appetite, while Basking shut his eyes upon the vision. He pressed on.

"The matter I spoke of, my lord, concerns a young relative of mine, whom I believe to be a particular friend of yours."

Something in the man's tone caught Brookmere's attention, and he looked up from his food expectantly.

"My distant cousin, Miss Alyssa Wentworth, has recently come into an inheritance from her late father, my great-uncle."

"Get to the point," snapped the viscount, whose expression had changed from curiosity to wariness at the mention of Miss Wentworth.

"Yes, well, to put it bluntly, my lord, she can only receive the inheritance if she marries a titled gentleman within the year. According to the will, if she cannot comply with these requirements, she will lose a considerable fortune, including a large property and indeed, her home."

"What the devil do you mean by coming to me with such a story?" demanded Brookmere, pounding the table with his fist so that the silverware jumped.

"I assure you it is true, sir." Basking flinched but stood his ground. "I myself was present when the will was read. A matter of an entail, I believe." He edged casually away from the angry viscount. "Apparently my cousin has requested her solicitor, a Mr. Nod or Noodle, or some such name, to assist her in complying with these terms. To that end the solicitor drew up, at her request, a list of—forgive me if I put it too crudely—prospective husbands." He noted with satisfaction Brookmere's look of distaste. "Along with pertinent information about each of them."

"What the devil has any of this to do with me?" Brookmere's voice was low and controlled, but he pushed away his half-full plate, all appetite banished.

By now Basking could not hide his pleasure in the viscount's discomfort. He produced the paper in question with a flourish. "Your name, my dear sir, was on it."

Brookmere tore it from his hand and read it quickly, his face darkening with rage. He stood up, towering over his unwelcome guest, and, with deceptive mildness that masked a fury tightly leashed, said, "Get out."

"But my lord, is this not valuable information? Are you not grateful to me for opening your eyes to the plotting of my cousin and protecting you from her scheme to entrap you?"

"I said get out, and don't ever come carrying such filthy tales about Miss Wentworth to me again."

"It is true! You have the proof in your hands."

The viscount was implacable. "I am going to destroy this, and if you don't leave immediately I will give in to the temptation to destroy you, as well. You are something less than a man, else I would demand that you name your friends."

He clenched his fists, struggling to clear his mind of rage and hurt. Finally he advanced on Basking, who shrank away. "I want to know only one thing. Who will inherit if Miss Wentworth is unable to fulfill the conditions?"

Basking only smiled and licked his lips nervously, eyeing his exit path. "I am sorry, my lord, that you do not find this information worth some reward. However, I am sure that there are others, perhaps acquaintances of yours, who would find it rather amusing. Although you may have the list and do with it what you will, I still retain the use of my tongue." He backed toward the door. "If you should happen to think better of it, please feel free to call upon me at Dunscombe, where I shall be secluded for a brief spell.

My health, you know...." With this he darted for the door.

Brookmere let him go, sat down heavily and put his head into his hands. It went against his nature to believe a lying fop like Henry Basking, but he could not deny the proof before his eyes. He scanned the list again, before tearing it to shreds. The woman he had been ready to love had turned out to be no more than the vulgar, middle-class heiress he had first thought her, despite her elegant ways.

It would not hurt so much if he had any suspicion that she might harbor the slightest affection for him. But there was no evidence, despite her sweetness last evening, that he was anything to her but the solution to her problem. Her eager response to his kiss he dismissed now as mere playacting.

Lord Brookmere grabbed a sheet of notepaper and penned a hurried, barely polite note of excuse. He slammed out of his town house a few hours later, and spent the rest of the morning at his club. In the afternoon, hoping that exercise would relieve the anger and tension that had only mounted as he brooded over the morning's events, he had his favorite hack saddled and rode to Hyde Park.

THAT MORNING at the house in Green Street, it had been Alyssa, for a change, who went about distracted. The memory of the previous evening refused to leave her, and she was amazed at her success in transforming a hostile, overbearing man into a gentleman whom she could think of with pleasure.

After an early service at St. George's, Hanover Square, Alyssa had nothing to do but think of him until the time of their afternoon engagement. *A month ago,* she thought standing before her dressing table, absently fingering her hair ribbons, *I would have gone into whoops if anyone had suggested that I might ever receive an invitation from Lord Brookmere.* The memories of everything they had ever said and done, especially the kiss, were beginning to take on a whole new meaning.

There was a tap at her door, and Nan put her head in, her frilled cap gone awry, her eyes gleaming. "Excuse me, miss, but Lord Selbridge inquires if you are at home. He is in the morning room." She was clearly impressed by this visit from someone of so high a rank.

Alyssa was startled at the news and uncertain. Although she had liked the earl immediately, she had not had the time or inclination to think of him. Still, she might as well have something to do other than wander about the house until her drive with Brookmere. If only she could keep her pulse from racing every time she thought of it!

The earl rose and smiled as she entered the room and gave him her hand. He really had a very charming smile, she thought, but he ought to be just a bit taller. . . .

"Good morning, Miss Wentworth. I hope I have not taken you away from anything important?"

"No, not at all," she assured him. *Unless,* she said to herself, *you consider daydreaming an essential activity.* "Will you take some refreshment? My aunt and stepmother are sure to return at any moment. I know they will be pleased to see you."

He shook his head regretfully. "Thank you, but my time, unfortunately, is not my own. I have an engagement in a quarter of an hour. I hope you will forgive me, Miss Wentworth, for coming by in this hurly-burly manner, but I really wanted to know if you would care to ride with me this afternoon. I could not help but notice last evening, when the subject arose, your interest in horses, and if you haven't your own here in town, I would be delighted to mount you from my own stables."

So he had overheard her conversation with Brookmere, she mused. She regarded him more carefully, and could not deny that she liked what she saw. However, she had no regrets at having to refuse the invitation. "I very much appreciate your asking, my lord, but I am afraid I—"

There was a discreet knock upon the open door, and Oliver stood on the threshold.

"I beg your pardon, miss, but there is a note for you. No reply is requested."

Alyssa excused herself and took the note. She broke the seal, wondering at the unfamiliar handwriting. As she scanned the contents, her spirits sank. It was from Brookmere. What could he mean, he was unable to keep their engagement? And there was no warmth or friendliness in the language. She puzzled over it for a moment, unaware that her visitor was watching with interest the play of emotions on her face.

Suddenly recalling his presence, she said, blushing, "Please forgive me—I had not meant to ignore you—it is only that—"

"No bad news, I trust?"

"No," she replied quickly, "not at all, in fact...."
She forced herself to smile. "In a way it is good news,
because I will be able to ride with you this afternoon,
after all."

The earl's eyes lit with pleasure and he soon took his
leave, keeping her hand a trifle too long as he told her
how much he looked forward to their ride.

She did not really pay attention. Her mind still ran
steadily on the contents of Brookmere's note.

When Selbridge was gone, she read it again and
again, as if there were a hidden message to be found
in the brief, cold lines. But she could find none.

At half-past three a subdued Alyssa made herself
ready for the ride, putting on a full-skirted amber
kerseymere habit, with ivory lace at the neck, a brown
beaver hat with a veil, and soft brown leather boots.
She was coming down the stairs, gloves and whip in
hand, when she heard the knocker and saw Oliver admit Lord Selbridge.

He looked up at her as she paused on the step, and
his eyes were full of admiration. For a fleeting moment she remembered in whose eyes she had hoped to
see that same expression, but she pushed the thought
aside and went down to greet him.

"I've brought you a chestnut mare I think you'll be
pleased with," he said as he escorted her out to where
the grooms stood holding the horses. "She's a sweet
goer, with the prettiest manners, but not lacking in
spirit. Much, in fact, like yourself, Miss Wentworth."

Alyssa had never before been compared to a horse.
Only someone like the earl could make such a pretty
compliment of it! She could not help but chuckle as

she thanked him, but he took no offense and only winked at her mischievously as he waved aside the groom and tossed her into the saddle.

The mare was everything Selbridge had claimed and Alyssa could not wait to try out her paces. At last they entered the park, avoiding the carriage drive, which, at this time of day, was crowded with society folk parading their finery and expensive equipages. They sought out a relatively uncrowded path, where, followed discreetly by a groom, they were soon able to put their horses to the trot.

Alyssa felt all the joy of riding again after being so long without the exercise. Soon she urged her mount past the earl, who was satisfied to let her go ahead of him, the better to admire her upright figure and elegant seat.

She was therefore momentarily alone when she slowed the mare to walk a few yards from a fork in the path. She was about to turn and look for Selbridge when, from a tree-lined path on the left, a large black gelding and his rider emerged. To the mutual embarrassment of both riders, they recognized each other too late to turn back.

Alyssa stared at Lord Brookmere helplessly. There were no words to express what she felt at his defection.

"I make no apology for canceling our engagement, Miss Wentworth," he said before she could speak. "I think I am the one due an apology. Deception does not become you."

His expression was disdainful, his voice cold as he addressed her, but she did not fail to note the pain in his eyes, and wonder at it. But she had no idea what he was talking about.

"I—I don't understand," she stammered helplessly. "Please explain."

His lip curled in contempt. "It is you who need to do the explaining. And not only to me, but to five other fortunate gentlemen. Perhaps one of them will oblige you, but you may cross off *my* name this instant." He wheeled his horse and rode back the way he had come.

Alyssa was trembling in the saddle, her hands clenching the reins so that the poor mare shifted uneasily beneath her.

How dare he... And then the full force of what he had said hit her and she would have fallen if she had not heard the sound of Selbridge riding up behind her. On no account must he know! She forced the tortured thoughts from her mind. She would puzzle it all out later, when she was alone, but Brookmere's implication was too clear to be missed. It was all because of that wretched list.

Lord Selbridge could not have known what had taken place. It had been so brief, and ended before he pulled his horse up next to Alyssa. But he could not have failed to notice her abstraction and the paleness of her cheeks, for he put himself out to be as charming and witty as possible.

Before they left the park, he had Alyssa laughing, albeit unwillingly, at his jests. Although unable to forget the look of contempt on Brookmere's face, she felt her spirits revive enough to be able to think kindly of the earl.

When he helped her to dismount before the house, he boldly allowed himself to hold her slim waist just a second longer than was necessary, and smiled into her eyes. She blushed and looked away, but he was satisfied with her reaction.

THE WENTWORTH LADIES made few calls the next day, and hurried home early to prepare for their dinner party. Alyssa was not surprised to find, upon her return, a note of excuse from the viscount, saying only that he had been called out of town and regretted not being able to attend. This one she did not reread, but merely tore it in two.

Clara, knowing nothing of the events of the day before, was justifiably annoyed. "I am very surprised at his lordship's bad manners, canceling at the last moment. That will leave us with uneven numbers, and we shall have to be equally rude and invite another gentleman on very short notice."

Alyssa timidly offered to send a note to Lord Selbridge. Clara raised her eyebrows at this, though she knew he had called on her stepdaughter, but made no objection. The note was sent, and to Clara's surprise, a gracious acceptance was returned.

While Alyssa was being helped into her evening dress of figured aquamarine silk, Clara knocked softly and entered her room.

"I'm sorry to disturb you while you are dressing, my love, but I need to speak with you alone before the guests arrive."

"I'm almost ready," she replied, sitting down to give Nan the opportunity to touch up her coiffure, and then dismissed the maid.

She turned to her stepmother, having a fairly good idea of what this visit portended. "What was it you wished to see me about, dearest?"

Clara flushed and lost some of her usual poise. "You see, my love, it is just that—that is, I hope you won't be offended, your dear father... it is rather too soon, I know, but it has all happened so unexpectedly...."

Alyssa could not restrain herself a moment longer. She jumped up and hugged her stepmother. "Let me be the first to wish you both be very happy. Sir Edward is a fine man, and no one who sees you together can doubt that he adores you."

Clara's amazement and relief was such that they both laughed until they were breathless. "Oh, Alyssa," she gasped, "you don't know how happy I am that you approve. Of course, it will not be for a while—it would not be seemly—but... surely I shall be married by next spring. I would not for the world wish you to think I was lacking in respect for your dear papa's memory."

"I would never think such a thing, you goose!"

Clara was glowing, but one more small doubt assailed her. "You know, my dear, at first I thought that Sir Edward—I mean that you and he might—"

"Oh, no, Clara, it was never like that. Of course I like him very much, but I think I knew almost from the first that—that he was not the one for me," she finished softly.

Clara only hugged her in silence, and they went down to greet their guests.

Among the first to arrive was Lady Pomeroy, and Alyssa dreaded facing her, for her great-aunt was sure to ask about the viscount. She knew that she would never be able to keep the truth from the old lady.

"Well, miss," Lady Pomeroy greeted her unceremoniously, "what did I tell you? That Brookmere fellow is the one, though Selbridge as much as told me that he was bowled over himself."

Alyssa took her great-aunt aside and miserably related the events of the previous day.

"Hmmph! What's come over the fellow? Demmed impertinence. I've half a mind to march straight over to his house and teach him not to treat any of my family in such a high-handed way. Deception, indeed! He ought to credit you with more sense."

"Oh, no, I beg of you, please do not do any such thing!"

Lady Pomeroy looked sharply at the horrified Alyssa, but only sniffed and admitted, "Can't do it, anyway. He's gone back to Brookmere. Heard it today and only thought he had gone to tell his mama the good news. Impudent young fool! Oh, he'll be back," she added, noting the distress on Alyssa's face, "but by then I hope you'll have accepted an offer from another admirer. Our fine viscount has disappointed me."

Alyssa could only agree silently, and then her attention was drawn to Selbridge, who had just entered and was obviously searching for her. With an encouraging nod and a sly wink, her ladyship left them together.

"I fear you will think it frightfully rude of us, my lord, but the truth is that one of our guests was obliged to—that is—" She was mortified at the necessity of revealing the truth to him. "Lord Brookmere was called away suddenly and I know it was presumptuous of me, but I thought of you and hoped you would be able to join us.''

Alyssa was quite flustered by the time she had managed to say this, for she was sure he had noticed her enjoyment of Brookmere's company at Lady Pomeroy's and knew of the sudden cancellation that had freed her to ride with him.

''I am honored that you did think of me, Miss Wentworth.'' And not too proud, he could have added, to take Brookmere's place at dinner if there was a chance that he might be able to replace him in Miss Wentworth's affections. ''Feel free to call upon me at need, as if I were already an old friend.'' His smile was warmer than ever.

Alyssa thanked him, still feeling guilty, and for the rest of the evening struggled to forget the viscount and make herself especially attentive to Selbridge. By the time the guests were ready to depart, Lady Pomeroy's sharp eyes could detect signs that the earl was already in a fair way to falling in love with her pretty niece.

Socially, the evening was a great success. The courses were plentiful and well prepared, the guests disposed to be pleased, and the three hostesses, despite their individual romantic preoccupations, succeeded in showing their London friends that they could entertain in style.

Yet Alyssa looked forward to further entertainments with all the enthusiasm one might reserve for the prospect of suffering a miserable cold in the head. Her social acceptance, so crucial to her plans, was a hollow victory. Though neither her conversation, nor her play at whist or upon the pianoforte betrayed it, her one desire was for the guests to leave so that she could throw herself upon her bed and cry.

Still, she forced herself to accept Selbridge's invitation to drive, as well as granting him a waltz at Lady Sefton's ball on Friday next, without which assurance he playfully refused to leave. By the time she escaped to her chamber, where she wearily allowed Nan to undress her, she was too overwrought even to cry.

I am so tired of pretending, she thought, drawing the bedclothes up to her chin. Tired of feigning happiness, gratitude and a heart untouched. The only way to protect herself from further hurt, she decided, would be to forget that Lord Brookmere existed, and to forget that she had ever been on the point of falling in love.

CHAPTER TWELVE

ALYSSA'S INCREASING social obligations left her little
time to brood about Lord Brookmere. Invitations began to arrive faster, and on some evenings the ladies
had to choose among three or more parties, or visit
more than one house in the course of an evening.

With each of their own entertainments in Green
Street, and the increasingly marked attentions of such
a personage as Lord Selbridge, the Wentworth ladies
gained the acceptance of even the highest sticklers of
the ton. The origins of their fortune, together with that
long ago runaway marriage, seemed to have been forgotten, and sooner than Alyssa had thought possible,
Clara was drawing up a guest list for a ball.

One fine June day Alyssa and her stepmother, both
owning themselves completely done up by the social
pace, decided to forgo their usual morning calls. With
Henrietta safely in the company of Lord Robert, they
denied themselves to callers and relaxed in their tiny,
but immaculately kept city garden.

Clara was embroidering, and Alyssa was reading
desultorily, her thoughts, as usual, straying to the
subject forbidden to them. They were interrupted
when Oliver, looking conscious of disobeying an order but convinced of the rightness of his action, came
into the garden and announced a caller who he was

sure madam had been mistaken in not instructing him to admit.

Alyssa, on the point of dozing off over her book due to the lulling effect of the warm sun on her neck, started and dropped her volume of poetry at the sight of the gentleman who followed Oliver. She fought to master her absurd disappointment and made herself greet Lord Selbridge calmly.

"Permit me to say that you ladies outshine even this bright weather and that you set off those roses behind you to perfection." As usual, he delivered the most effusive compliments in a self-mocking manner, but Alyssa knew from the light in his eyes that he was sincere.

She smiled, but let Clara thank him for the compliment. She was beginning to feel guilty about him, for he called on her almost every day and she rode or drove with him several times a week. The haut ton observed all this with interest, and more than one sharp-eyed matron was scanning the morning paper for that announcement that would put an end to all speculation.

Even Clara had teasingly said to her stepdaughter, "And how shall you like being a countess, my love? Will you still acknowledge your poor stepmother though she is only to be Lady Talbot?"

To Alyssa's relief, the earl had made no offer, but his behavior made it apparent he was coming closer to it every day. She dreaded the decision she must make.

She liked and respected him too much to deceive him as to her feelings. To refuse him would defeat the entire purpose of her coming to town, but she could not buy her inheritance at the cost of her conscience.

It would be another thing altogether if he, too, wanted a convenient marriage, but his feelings were apparent and it was a love match he sought.

When Clara suddenly discovered she had not her embroidery scissors with her Alyssa could not protest, though she had seen them in Clara's hand not five minutes before. Reluctantly, she allowed her stepmother to leave her alone with the earl.

They stood and looked at the roses, and chatted idly for a few minutes of the fine weather, of their acquaintance, of the week's coming events. But underneath their polite conversation lay a tension that Alyssa could feel as though it were a rushing spring confined underground, seeking to burst out into a bubbling fountain.

At length a gap in their conversation provided the opportunity. Seating himself close beside her on a sunwarmed stone bench and enfolding her hand in his, the earl very tenderly expressed his love and asked her to be his wife.

Alyssa was silent for a long moment, but the look in his eyes told her what she must do. "My lord," she said unsteadily, looking away now because of the pain she knew she would see in his face, "I want you to know that I am aware of the great honor you do me, and I shall always be grateful to you for it and hope to retain your respect and friendship. The truth is that though I have the greatest liking and respect for you, I—" She could not finish, for there was a lump in her throat.

"You do not think you can love me," Selbridge ended it for her with a deep sigh of regret, and released her hand. "I understand, Miss Wentworth—

Alyssa—truly I do, and it was not out of confidence that you returned my affection that I asked you to marry me, but only in the hope that one day you could learn to love me."

Alyssa looked up at him helplessly. He had been a good friend to her, but she could not reveal, not even to spare him hurt, that which until this moment she had refused to admit to herself. She loved Lord Brookmere.

If she had not already given her heart to the viscount, perhaps even as long ago as their ridiculous encounter in Swinbury, she would have had no qualms about becoming the countess of Selbridge and in one stroke securing her inheritance and a loving husband. But it was too late.

Henrietta and Clara were shocked when they learned she had refused the earl's offer. They could not believe that she would not regret her decision, but as the day went on, Alyssa began to feel as though a burden had been lifted from her heart. If not cheerful, she was at least serene, for at last she knew her own mind.

Another person to whom the news came as a surprise was Lady Pomeroy, who heard it by some mysterious means involving her dresser, her coachman, Mrs. Wentworth's second parlormaid and Miss Munsen, who was the ultimate bearer of the tale the next day.

"What's that you say, Althea? Speak up, gel. You're mumbling again. She's refused Selbridge? Hmmph! It's worse than I thought, then. Should have accepted him. That would've made his lordship come out of hiding fast enough. He hasn't been seen in town in weeks."

Miss Munsen ventured to speak. "My lady, it is said that Lord Brookmere returned to town just yester-day.'

Her ladyship smiled and, tossing aside her netting, called for her walking stick, bonnet and gloves, and ordered her carriage to be brought round at once.

Brookmere had indeed arrived in London the day before. Much as he loved his home, he could not bear the tedium of being alone for so long. He had invited no guests to share his self-imposed exile, for in his grim mood he was no fit company for even his closest friends. Days of riding over his lands and long evenings over a book and a bottle of brandy could not banish the memory of a pair of reproachful green eyes in a shocked white face.

Back in his town house, he went through the stack of cards and invitations on his desk. He paused for a moment over a card addressed from Green Street for a ball to be given the next evening by Mrs. Clara Wentworth. His face darkened and he was about to discard the invitation, when his butler announced the arrival of a caller, the Lady Elizabeth Pomeroy.

AS EARLY AS SEVEN O'CLOCK the next morning, the Wentworth house was in a most pleasant confusion in preparation for the ball. The double drawing rooms with tall windows overlooking the garden were emptied of furniture, the rugs rolled up and taken to the attics and the floor polished until it would reflect the light of the hundreds of candles in the two huge crystal chandeliers. Small gilt chairs were set against the wall for the matrons and the unpartnered ladies.

In a smaller adjacent room, three long tables were placed against one wall for punch and lemonade, while the kitchen staff procured tubs of ice to chill the champagne that would be served by circulating footmen. In addition there would be all sorts of delicacies to feast upon.

Henrietta, scurrying about her bedchamber, thought of the sweets and her mouth watered, but she told herself that there would be other balls to attend and other buffets to enjoy.

Today, she reminded herself sternly, was too special for mere eating. She was sorry to miss the ball, to which she had been looking forward since leaving Finchwood, but there was nothing else to be done.

She had finally convinced her beloved Lord Norton to carry her off to Gretna Green, and with all the confusion in the house, today was the best day to do it. With luck, she would not be missed until late afternoon, and by then it would be too late for anyone to overtake them before dark.

She had breakfast very early in her room, and told her maid that she had the headache and would not be coming downstairs, as she wished to be rested and well for the ball. She scribbled a note to her sister-in-law and niece and left it on the mantel.

Dressing quickly in what was, for her, an inconspicuous gown of coquelicot muslin, and donning a leghorn bonnet trimmed with violet ribbons and a heavy lace veil, she fled down the servants' stair, carrying a bandbox crammed full of colorful dresses.

There in a nearly deserted side street Lord Norton's chaise awaited her.

It was actually well before the afternoon that Henrietta's absence was discovered. After an early luncheon, Alyssa took a tray up to her aunt, who was not accustomed to have the headache, and certainly not to spend the entire morning in bed without eating.

The disarray of the room, the empty bed, the note on the mantel all made Alyssa's heart lurch with fear. When she recognized her aunt's handwriting, she rejected her first wild notion that her poor Henrietta had fallen victim to an abductor.

The note, much stained with tears, begged them not to worry and to forgive her for spoiling the ball. Miss Norton's conduct was pronounced to be outrageous and the only remedy for it was a wedding over the anvil. Perhaps they could tell everyone she was called away to Bath to see a sick friend.

Alyssa did not know whether to laugh or cry. The idea of a middle-aged woman and her dull suitor, who were not by any means prevented from marrying, except perhaps in their imaginations, running off to the border as though they were youngsters whose parents had forbidden their union, was ludicrous. It was an appalling parody of the marriage of her parents, who had faced true and insurmountable impediments in their search for happiness.

She could not help but wonder if by this foolish action her aunt had finally pushed herself over the edge of respectability. So far she had been tolerated by the fashionable world because of the popularity of her niece and Clara, but the ton had always looked askance at her. Once word of this ridiculous escapade reached the ears of the leaders of the beau monde, it was likely they would lose all respect for the Wentworths.

With a guilty start, Alyssa recollected that she ought to be thinking of her aunt's safety and happiness instead of her own consequence. She hurried to show the note to Clara.

"I will leave immediately," she told her horrified stepmother, "and with luck, I will be able to overtake them at some point along the North Road."

"You will do no such thing!" cried Clara. "I forbid you to leave the house. How can you think of driving off alone after them? Besides, if you do we shall have to cancel the ball." She clutched at Alyssa's arm as if to keep her from leaving. "I would cancel it in a moment if I thought it would do any good, but it would cause the most horrid scandal, and that we must avoid, especially for your sake."

Alyssa recognized the truth of it all, but stood firm.

"Clara, I must go. Surely you can see that? I'll take a groom or a footman with me, or even Nan, but Henrietta and Lord Norton must be brought back before they spend a night on the road. Besides, you'll not have to cancel the ball. You can tell everyone that Henrietta was called away to Bath—that's one of the most useful suggestions she's ever made—and that I am in bed with a fever. No one need hear about the elopement."

"Now I must hurry, for there is no time to be lost." She was tying her bonnet strings as she spoke, when Oliver announced the Viscount Brookmere.

Alyssa spun to face the door, ready to say that she would not receive him, but he was already in the room.

He took in the scene, and without allowing the flushed and angry Alyssa to speak, went to her and took her hand. The sudden warm pressure of his flesh startled her, and she hesitated long enough for him to address her.

"I came here to say something particular to you, but it appears that this is an inconvenient time. Is there some way in which I can assist you? I am willing to do what I can, whatever it may be."

Alyssa, regaining her poise, was about to reply scathingly that she could do very well without *his* help, when Clara forestalled her by going to him at once and telling him the entire story.

Brookmere listened silently, only raising his eyebrows a fraction when he heard what Henrietta had done. He pulled the watch out of his waistcoat pocket, consulted it and said, "It's now half-past one. If we leave immediately we can overtake them long before dark. Norton's so cowhanded that even your aunt could handle the ribbons better than he, though he wouldn't have the sense to give them to her. I think you'll find that we'll have no trouble catching up to them." He smiled with engaging confidence.

Alyssa, on hearing this, took her pelisse, reticule and gloves and, ignoring Clara's protests, asked Lord Brookmere if he had any idea how long the journey would take.

"If all goes well, and there's no reason why it should not, we will overtake them by late afternoon. We shall take a room at a posting house for you and Miss Wentworth, and I'll ring a peal over Norton for agreeing to such a crackbrained scheme. Tomorrow we'll see the lovers safely home, where they can be married in proper style."

"All right, then, let us go now, please. In spite of what you say, I cannot rest easy until I am on my way." She turned to reassure Clara. "Don't worry, we shall bring Henrietta home no later than tomorrow, and if you keep your head tonight, as I know you will, no one will be the wiser."

Clara looked at Brookmere uncertainly. "Are you quite sure, my love?" she asked her stepdaughter.

His lordship turned a gentle smile on the anxious lady. "I promise you, no harm will come to her. My word as man of honor."

Clara looked into his eyes and was apparently satisfied with what she saw there, for she made no further objections.

In a shorter time than she would have imagined possible, Alyssa found herself out of the crowded streets and on the road leading north. So far she had exchanged not a word with the viscount that did not immediately concern their journey. It was only now that she realized with a start that they were completely alone, for his lordship was unattended by a groom, and all the awkwardness of her situation was brought home to her. Then, too, if they should happen to be seen driving alone on the road north... Resolutely she put these anxieties behind her and concentrated on the present.

"How far can these bays of yours take us?" she asked. "It would not do to have to hire post-horses. How horrid to have a postboy along on such an errand!"

"The bays are fresh and good for two stages. By then we may have caught up with our quarry. If not...." He glanced at her ruefully. "If I were as wealthy as you, my dear, I should no doubt have my own horses stabled at convenient posting houses on all the main roads, and we should not have to worry about inquisitive postboys. However, we shall contrive."

This awakened her slumbering antagonism. "How do you know how wealthy I am?"

"I beg your pardon, but I was not aware that the extent of the Wentworth fortune was any secret now that you are out in society. Besides, your great-aunt, Lady Pomeroy, was so kind as to pay me a visit yesterday."

"Aunt Elizabeth!" cried Alyssa in horror. "What—what did she say to you?"

"Much that was of great interest to me," Brookmere replied, keeping his eyes on the road, "We had a very enlightening talk."

"She had no right—indeed, sir, it is no business of yours to know all my personal circumstances." Did Aunt Elizabeth still believe that she loved him, and had she suggested—

"Did I say she had revealed anything of a personal nature?" he inquired blandly. "Have no fear, Lady Pomeroy said nothing that was not to your credit. Though you are going about things in a rather unusual way. I admit that when that fellow Basking first revealed your plan to me I was grossly insulted. However, her ladyship made me see the error of my ways."

These revelations did nothing to soothe Alyssa's temper. "Did she really, my lord? And how considerate of my cousin Basking to inform you of my...plan," she said with deceptive calm.

In the excitement over Henrietta's disappearance she had almost forgotten the theft of the list, and the reminder that her cousin had shown it to Lord Brookmere was enough to make her cry. But his lordship's nonchalant attitude stiffened her resolve to show him she could not be pacified so easily.

"Well, my dear," he continued, "you can scarcely suppose a gentleman would be flattered to find himself on a list of eligible bachelors, destined to be the savior of a disagreeably circumstanced heiress who is under pressure of time to marry a title. One would prefer to be sought after for one's own endearing qualities." He smiled wryly at her, but she was in no mood to be cajoled.

"You are overconfident, my lord," she said coldly, suppressing her pangs of loss. "Neither your title nor your so-called endearing qualities are in any demand by *this* heiress. You are mistaken if you believe that anything you say, after the insult to which you subjected me, could improve my opinion of you one whit."

"It is you who are mistaken, Miss Wentworth," he retorted, stung by her words. "Your encouragement of my attentions at Lady Pomeroy's that evening misled me into believing that I was the one to be honored with your choice. I must inform you that I have no intention of putting my title to such a use. I am no fortune hunter."

"Is that so, sir?" Despite the import of his words, Alyssa was pleased to see his coolness disappear. He lost concentration long enough to cause a near mishap with a passing wagon.

"I find I cannot oblige you by believing your assertion, else why did you come to me today, apparently eager to make up for your past behavior and to return to my good graces? Futile, I assure you, for you are everything—" her voice faltered "—everything I mean to avoid in a husband."

She saw him grip the reins so tightly that his knuckles whitened, and the poor horses were thrown into an irritable prance. After restoring them to order he said with barely suppressed contempt, "Very well, then, Miss Wentworth, I shall no longer burden you with my conversation."

Alyssa's pride prevented her from letting him have the last word, and foreseeing a journey of extreme discomfort, she announced that she would be obliged if he would set her down at the next posting house, where she would continue on her own.

Too late she realized how foolish this sounded. A young lady, unaccompanied, driving on a main road and inquiring along the way for a runaway couple, was sure to be subjected to a vast amount of unpleasantness or even danger.

Brookmere did not intend to be cruel, but he could not help laughing in genuine amusement at the expression of dismay that crossed Alyssa's face as soon as the words were out.

"Just what do you find so amusing, my lord? Do you think I could not drive myself to the border if I chose? I assure you I am quite as competent as yourself."

His grin exasperated her. "That's fortunate. If I tire and want to rest my eyes, I can leave the reins to you and trust you not to overturn us into a ditch."

Her fury at this found solace only in the act of ignoring him for the next hour.

CHAPTER THIRTEEN

LORD BROOKMERE BROKE the chilly silence only when they reached a posting house, where, he maintained, they ought to seek news of the runaways.

This Alyssa was eager to do, as well as to stretch her legs and eat a bit of bread and ham, but they faced a grave setback in the information provided by the chief hostler of the establishment. This individual, squinting cannily at the coins offered by Lord Brookmere, shook his head and gave it as his opinion that if the lady with the red dress and the gentleman with the red face were to reach their destination before getting into a regular mill, he'd give up his ale for a month.

"What's this? Have they been quarreling? Oh, poor Aunt Henrietta!"

"Rather, poor Norton," commented his lordship dryly. "Would you be able to give us an idea of what o'clock they continued north?" he inquired of the hostler.

"No, sir, I wouldn't at that." But at Brookmere's sighing and reaching for his purse once more, his informant waved a leathery hand. "Not, milord, that you ain't come up with enough to jog my mem'ry. It's that they didn't keep on this road. They didn't go north, or not by any route I'd take."

Alyssa and Brookmere exchanged a bewildered glance.

"Wherever could they be planning to go, if not to Gretna?" she asked.

Brookmere only shook his head and questioned the man more closely. "Did they happen to mention their destination?"

"They didn't rightly have none." The weathered worthy of the post roads seemed to be taking a perverse pleasure in amazing his audience. At the rising impatience in the viscount's expression, however, he hastily amended his report.

"The leddy was afraid of summat—I don't rightly know what. She commences to weep, until her lord agrees to ride off the post road and tie up for the night at some little village, unknown like. Told 'em they wanted the Three Feathers, just past Battford."

"And did they go?" demanded Alyssa.

He looked at her reproachfully. "Said so, didn't I?" He made as if to walk but, as an afterthought, said over his shoulder, "You want to follow 'em, you takes the side road after the village for two, three miles, and then follow the signpost on the lane to Battford."

"Depend upon it," Alyssa said to Brookmere, her anger at him momentarily forgotten. "Aunt Henrietta has convinced herself that Miss Norton has had them followed, and means to spend the night away from the post road in order to elude pursuers. They probably intend to continue north in the morning, if I know my aunt, at cockcrow. Poor Lord Norton, indeed!"

"Of all the ridiculous starts!" Brookmere slapped his whip against his buckskinned thigh. "And the poor fellow didn't even think to grease the hostler in the fist to keep mum about it. Well, it only makes it a simpler matter than ever.''

He helped her back into the curricle and, glancing at the lowering sky, shook his head. ''No harm, I suppose, but I don't like those clouds and I don't like these country lanes.''

Luck was not with them, for after making good progress on the road indicated by their informant, they searched in vain for the signpost to Battford. Numerous lanes darted off on either side of the road, none of them marked. The sky was murky, and several ominous flashes of lightning streaked across it before the rumbles of thunder gathered themselves into a stupendous crack that sent the high-strung horses into a panic-filled rear. All the skill of even a noted whip like Brookmere could not calm them in time to prevent the curricle from tipping onto its side.

Alyssa found herself tossed out into a hedge, from which she emerged uninjured except for a few scratches. His lordship, equally unhurt, had rolled to his feet with the grace of an acrobat and was already at the horses' heads. He spared a glance for Alyssa, and observing that she was uninjured, commanded her to help him. Soon the animals were standing quite still before the wreck of their tangled harness and a toppled curricle with a broken axle.

At the very moment of their accident the rain had begun, and it now pelted down with such insistence that the plume on Alyssa's bonnet drooped sadly over her shoulder, while his lordship's lapels streamed with water on either side of his soggy neckcloth.

"We must get to shelter," Alyssa gasped, brushing the water out of her face as it ran into her eyes.

"An excellent suggestion." Her companion bore this new hardship with an unruffled calm that made her want to scream. She clenched her hands and took a watery breath, then set to work helping him to free the horses from the mess.

From his eminence of some six feet, Lord Brookmere spied an edifice of some sort not far down the muddy lane to their right. A few minutes of soggy trudging, leading the horses, found them in the yard of an ancient, rambling inn whose walls of moss-covered stone must have once looked on more prosperous times before new roads were laid out and traffic diverted away.

"Is this the Three Feathers?" Alyssa's voice held renewed hope. "We may yet find Aunt Henrietta."

Sadly, as they approached, his lordship made out a swinging sign in faded gray, once white, of a bird bearing some resemblance to a dove, and not a stray feather or plume to be seen.

The identity of this hostelry was confirmed when a wiry groom, summoned in the midst of a rainswept dash from the tumbledown stables to the side door, informed Brookmere that he was in the village of Paynton, that the inn was indeed the Dove and that the Three Feathers was three miles in the opposite direction, ushering them into the shelter of the inn.

"Our carriage has overturned on the road," the viscount informed the groom as they scurried into the dank, flagged hall. "Can we hire another here?"

"No," was the reply, and with that single word Alyssa's newly raised hopes were dashed yet again.

"We don't keep no veehickles for hire." With this he shuffled off to attend to the horses.

As he did so a stout, red-faced individual in a clean but wrinkled apron emerged from a door at the end of the hall, bringing with him the scent of spilled ale and pipe smoke. Catching sight of the arrivals, he bustled over as fast as his short legs would carry him.

"I am Ormsby, the proprietor, my lord," he said genially, rubbing his hands in true landlordly fashion. "How might I serve you and your lady?"

Brookmere did not correct him, for with the coming of the storm he had a disagreeable suspicion that before the day was over it would be necessary to have the landlord believe that Miss Wentworth was indeed his lady. He explained their dilemma, and the landlord confirmed that there were no vehicles of any type to be hired at the Dove.

"I am sorry, my lord," he continued, having no idea of the quality gentleman's rank but feeling it was preferable to err on the side of generosity, "but we don't get much custom from the great road. It's all local traffic here. However, my wife and I will be happy to make you and her ladyship comfortable. If it would please your lordship to step into my best parlor, where we can have a fire going—"

They were soon ensconced in a small, but comfortable room, warming themselves before the grate. While Alyssa was removing her wet pelisse, Brookmere ordered dinner and, to Alyssa's astonishment, a bedchamber.

Before she could say a word, the landlord's wife came to wait on her and escorted her upstairs, where she might repair her appearance. The landlady was obviously in awe of her elegant guest and handled her pelisse and bonnet reverently.

Then she looked proudly around at the plain but comfortable room, sure that her visitor could find no fault with the handmade rugs, the curtains of bleached linen and the huge bed with its fluffy, quilted coverlet. "If you'll pardon me for saying so, my lady, I do believe you and his lordship would be very comfortable here if you was wishful to spend the night. Even if we send a man to see to your carriage when the rain stops, the road'll be no more than mud, and it'll be coming on dark, with no moon tonight."

"Thank you, Mrs. Ormsby, but we must find some way to continue on our journey. Is there not another place in the village where we might hire a carriage?"

"No, my lady, none that I know of."

Alyssa mentally reminded herself to speak to Brookmere about this "my lady" matter. As for staying here with him, it was of course impossible. She was not so naive as to suppose her reputation could stand such a scandal. She went downstairs determined to confront him on several points.

As she joined him again in the parlor, his eyes widened in pleasure, for the firelight cast a golden glow on her skin and her hair was curling of its own accord in the humid air. Her leaf-green muslin gown, brushed free of the dirt from her fall, was still slightly damp, and clung to her waist and hips in a most revealing way. She stood warming her hands before the flames and did not return his gaze.

"My dear Miss Wentworth—or should I say Lady Brookmere? I hope the bedchamber is to your liking.

It looks very much as though we shall be spending the night at this rustic place.''

She whirled to face him, her emerald eyes glinting dangerously. ''How dare you pretend that we are man and wife! I refuse to stay here with you. Even if we cannot get the chaise repaired tonight there must be some inhabitant of this village with a conveyance we can hire.''

Suddenly she was alarmed, for he had taken a step toward her and now towered over her, so that she had to put her head back just to see his face. Unwilling to be dominated thus by the unfair advantage of mere height, she had a sudden wild thought of treading on his foot.

He smiled down at her as if reading her mind. ''And do you really think we should get as far again as the road in all this rain, possibly by farm cart? I assure you, we are not likely to find any better conveyance in this place. You must realize, my dear, that it is necessary for us to pose as a married couple here, just as it will be necessary, when we return to London, to announce our betrothal.''

Alyssa had not until this moment fully absorbed the serious nature of her situation. Here she saw, a lady unescorted even by a maid, alone at a secluded inn with a gentleman whose intentions toward her were questionable. That she knew she loved him, in spite of everything, was immaterial. Indeed, to the gossiping tongues of London, it would have only made their behavior seem more shocking.

She had spent enough time in town to know that nothing could remain a secret for long. If no one had seen them driving out of the city together, then someone might still see them returning the next day, which would be infinitely worse.

She knew in her heart that Brookmere was right, but all she could say was, "And what of Aunt Henrietta?"

"My dear, which do you think is more important? To preserve the good name of a young lady like yourself, who is highly regarded in society, or to risk it by continuing on an impossible pursuit of a foolish middle-aged couple who have eloped for no other reason than that it is romantic?" His eyes were not without pity.

Still, she could not give in so easily. He doesn't give a fig for me, she told herself. It would be the biggest mistake of my life to marry him this way. "Sir, I must ask you to remember that Miss Wentworth is my aunt, and though she may not be the most sensible person in the world—"

"Exactly. Therefore no one could think any more ill of her than they do now, knowing her, er, eccentricities."

Alyssa felt that if she were ten years younger she might have stamped her foot and pouted with frustration.

"It is so refreshing to see the Miss Wentworth I once knew and to hear her defend her family to me once more." Lord Brookmere had folded his arms and observed her change of expression with great amusement.

This did not make her feel any more charitable toward either him or his plan. She continued to argue that they must attempt to hire a carriage or wagon from one of the villagers, for there were several hours of light left.

"We may yet find them at the Three Feathers and perhaps bring them to a posting house where we can spend the night in an unexceptionable manner. Then we can dispense with this nonsensical form of a betrothal."

"No."

Alyssa clenched her fists and suppressed a desire to beat them on his broad chest. "Then take me back to London. If you so object to rescuing my aunt, then you should never have—"

"I am sorry you are so offended at the thought of it, Miss Wentworth, but as I know you to be a sensible female, surely you must realize that it is impossible. If you think I would hitch my beautiful bays to a farm cart, even if we could get one, which I doubt—"

"Oh . . . to the devil with your bays!" cried Alyssa, extremely provoked, and clapped a hand over her mouth immediately, turning bright pink.

Brookmere looked as though he were about to burst into laughter, but turned away, and when he turned back his face was serious. "You are overwrought," he said, taking her arm and bringing her closer to the fire. "When you think about it clearly you will see that it would not do. I am certainly not about to send some poor wretch tramping about the countryside in this storm to find me a wagon in which we will only get stuck on some muddy lane, far from even such rudimentary comforts as this old place offers."

"But my lord—"

"Enough!" His face was tightly drawn, his voice implacable.

The proprietor and his wife now entered with their meal, and it was a strain for Alyssa to appear calm until they had lifted the covers and gone. The viscount sniffed appreciatively, as unconcerned as if he had been cozily ensconced in his club. He held the chair for Alyssa and his fingers brushed her nape casually.

Her skin tingled and her pulses leaped. She could not enjoy a bit of the delicious dinner. She put down her fork to continue the discussion, only to be forestalled.

"I suggest that you try some of this excellent chicken," his lordship said firmly, "and may I pour you a glass of this claret?" He went on about the courses and the wines and ignored all her attempts to redirect the conversation, until she gloomily turned to her food, temporarily defeated.

"I wonder," he said, replacing his empty glass on the scrubbed table, "just what you find so objectionable in the fact that we must marry. I would think you'd be glad of it. Your worries will be at an end. You will have your titled husband and your inheritance. It is quite convenient." He observed her rising color and went on deliberately, "In fact, my arriving this afternoon to assist you was almost heaven-sent. Though how could you have known that our chase would end this way?"

"You insult me, sir." Alyssa threw down her napkin and stood, pushing her chair back so hard that it toppled to the floor. "No doubt you think me a scheming, shameless female, merely because I had the good sense to know I must fight for my inheritance. I abhor passivity."

"One could not say that you are other than a lady of action," he murmured.

"However," she said, ignoring him, "you will do me the honor of believing that my machinations, as you see them, did not include inducing my poor aunt to stage an elopement for the express purpose of my maneuvering you into a delicate situation. I should not dream of marrying a man who would believe me capable of such a thing. I would rather lose Finchwood forever. I know I shall always have a home with Sir Edward and Clara."

"Or with Lord Norton and Miss Henrietta," he reminded her, laughing at her over a fresh glass of wine.

"Oh, you are intolerable!" The man obviously did not care who he was obliged to bestow his name upon. No doubt he would take up with his Cyprians and opera dancers the moment the vows were exchanged.

"If I have to remain on the shelf for the rest of my days, and even if I am shunned by society for this one awful night, I still should not marry you!"

His lordship's amusement dissolved, and his eyes darkened in displeasure. He rose and moved swiftly around the table, grasped her chin and made her look into his eyes. "Listen to me, Miss Wentworth," he said softly but with unmistakable emphasis, "the facts are these. You are alone with me here, and whether anything untoward takes place between us or not, we have only to return to town together after a night spent away for people to believe that it has."

She was lost in his eyes and enthralled by his voice, and found that she did not want to protest when his arm came around her shoulders, drawing her closer. She breathed in his strangely stirring scent and quieted that tiny voice within that said she should break away.

"Tomorrow, immediately upon our return, I will place notice in the *Morning Post* announcing our engagement. You may tell your stepmother whatever you wish, but we shall say to everyone else that we have been secretly betrothed and were only waiting for my return to town to announce it."

He stroked her velvety cheek and tucked a stray curl behind her ear, and she felt her lips begin to tremble. The heat of his body penetrated her thin muslin gown and she thought that if he did not stop looking into her eyes her legs would collapse under her altogether. She was afraid and yet eager.

He saw the apprehension in her eyes and laughed softly. "Don't be afraid, my dear. I'll ask the landlord for another room tonight. I wouldn't presume to exercise my rights as a husband before the wedding night, whatever else we may have to pretend."

Now both his arms were tight around her and she was free to look away, but found she could not. Her breath was caught in her throat, and her heart pounded so hard that she was sure he must feel it.

He bent his head and whispered, "But I shall not hesitate to seal our betrothal right now," and pressed his mouth to hers.

His lips tasted of wine and were soft and gentle on hers. This time she was sure of her feelings, though not his, and the power of her emotions made her return his embrace with an ardor that shocked her.

Passion-swept as she was, she thought only hazily that she could not allow this to go on, that his feelings for her went no further than this, and soon the outside world began to intrude on her again.

She heard the crackling of the fire in the grate, a sudden loud noise from the taproom and footsteps in the hall. As if sensing her distraction, the viscount began to release her, just as an embarrassed Mr. Ormsby entered the room, clearing his throat self-consciously.

Alyssa turned away in shame, though she knew the landlord could not think it terribly odd that a lady should be kissed occasionally by her own husband. Yet her hands were very unsteady as she stood before the mirror over the sideboard and pushed back the strands of hair that had fallen loose.

Mr. Ormsby inquired if they would care for coffee, or cheese and fruit, his eyes darting from one to the other of his guests in burning curiosity.

"Coffee, please, and bring a bottle of brandy with it. Her ladyship will take some in her coffee to help her sleep. She is not feeling quite the thing and I'm afraid I shall have to trouble you for another bedchamber."

"Not at all, my lord. It shall be ready by the time you have done with your coffee," the host assured them. Seeing his mysterious guests in a passionate embrace had shaken his faith, for he had spent many years as a butler to the quality and knew that no self-respecting married couple engaged in such public displays of affection. But he was reassured by the request for another bedchamber. No husband and wife of the quality, he had observed, ever appeared to sleep in the same room.

Painfully aware of her renewed vulnerability and burdened with the knowledge that she had once again allowed a man who felt nothing for her to take immense liberties, Alyssa turned to Brookmere with an assurance she did not quite feel.

"I am perfectly well, thank you, and I do not care for any brandy. I shall go up to my room now." She moved toward the door, and when he put a detaining hand on her shoulder, she shook it off before her knees could turn to water again.

"Do not touch me. If you think because I have been so weak as to let my—my baser nature overcome my virtue that it will make it any easier to convince me to marry you, you are mistaken. I meant what I said, and I shall not marry you merely because of some absurd convention. You may put all the announcements in all the newspapers you like, but I shall deny it to everyone."

Brookmere dropped his hand abruptly. "Then, Miss Wentworth, you should not only make yourself appear a fool, but me, as well, and that I will not tolerate. Be sure you understand this. We shall announce our engagement tomorrow and before too much time has passed we will be married. You may be expert in deceiving yourself, my dear, but you cannot deceive me. I flatter myself that you will not find your wifely duties intolerable," he said coldly.

Alyssa gasped at his effrontery and, drawing away, said in a frigid voice, "I have deceived myself in nothing, sir, except perhaps in not realizing from the first that your insistence on this marriage shows that you are no more than a fortune hunter."

After one glimpse of his countenance slowly filling with rage, she fled the parlor and ran up the narrow wooden stairs to her chamber, holding in her sobs till the door was firmly shut behind her.

CHAPTER FOURTEEN

MORNING SUNLIGHT filtering through the curtains awakened Alyssa, and for a few moments she could not recall how she came to be sleeping in her shift in this plain little room, with its ancient whitewashed walls. She sat up and with a rush it all came back to her, and she could not stifle a groan.

She wondered if she ought to order breakfast in her room, but dismissed the idea. That was the coward's way out, she told herself. It hurt dreadfully to know how little Brookmere must think of her and that she could not help loving him, but she must continue to face him while planning how to extricate herself from this travesty of a betrothal.

When she came down Brookmere was already seated and had begun his meal. He merely nodded and poured her a cup of coffee. His face was a study in indifference, and he did not even trouble to speak of commonplaces, but finished his breakfast and rose.

"I have already been to see the blacksmith and he has promised that the curricle will be ready by noon. We will leave soon after."

"I will be ready." She met his glance with as much poise as she could muster. Brookmere left the parlor without another word, and she did not see him for the rest of the morning.

After her breakfast, she attempted to alleviate her boredom by playing patience with a greasy deck of cards she found in a corner cupboard. But worries about her own and her aunt's situation continually rose to plague her. She became restless and went to the door several times, until customers in the taproom began to stare. Then she confined herself to looking out the window.

The anticipation of a long journey beside the silent, unsmiling Brookmere depressed her spirits considerably, but she felt only relief when she was finally rewarded by the sight of the mended curricle being hauled up to the Dove. In a moment Lord Brookmere appeared from the stables, and after glancing over the vehicle, he turned toward the inn.

When he entered the parlor she was sitting placidly at the table with the cards spread before her. "The curricle is repaired and the horses are well rested," he said, his face expressionless. "We shall have something to eat and return to town."

After a brief and unnervingly silent meal, Brookmere helped his companion into the curricle, dropping her hand as if it were a live coal as soon as her feet touched the step. He had evidently paid the Ormsbys well, for they looked pleased and bade their guests a very attentive farewell, waving at the curricle till it had bowled out of sight toward the road.

Alyssa stole a sideways glance at him as they turned out of the lane onto the road. He looked back at her and seemed about to speak, but apparently thinking better of it, turned away without saying a word. He no longer looked angry, but he did look as though nothing she could say would ever change his mind about her.

Not, she assured herself, that she had anything to apologize for. It was his own behavior and insistence on the betrothal that had caused her to accuse him of wanting her fortune. He had not troubled to deny it. If he had any feelings for her, he must have expressed them long since. She could never marry him this way, and almost began to wish that she had accepted Selbridge's offer.

The solution struck her with a sudden blazing clarity. She felt she knew the characters of both gentlemen well enough to predict what would happen. Brookmere might prove a little difficult, but if she remained firm he would have to give in, and Selbridge... It would be delicate and embarrassing, but the attempt must be made if she were not to suffer by this silly accident for the rest of her life.

Though they spoke barely a dozen words to each other, the return journey passed swiftly for both travelers. The viscount kept his eyes on the road and his mind on unraveling the tangle his own carelessness had involved him in.

Alyssa brooded on a similar subject, also keeping her gaze fixed firmly on the road. When they entered the city, she could not help but glance anxiously about for fear that someone known to them would see a rather unkempt Lord Brookmere and Miss Wentworth driving together when they had both been conspicuous by their absence at Mrs. Wentworth's ball the night before.

Luckily, it was the hour of the day when ladies shopped or paid visits and when gentleman lounged in

Bond Street or took refuge in their clubs. Alyssa did not see a single face she knew, and relaxed a bit as they drew closer to home, only to feel Brookmere suddenly tense beside her.

She followed his glance and, to her absolute horror, saw none other than Henry Basking riding toward them. His eyes gleamed as he took in their disheveled appearance. The viscount, stubble cheeked, his neckcloth tied in a drooping approximation of his usual style, his boots with less than their customary mirror finish, glared at him until he looked away.

Alyssa sat beside him in her wrinkled gown, her hair falling out of its pins beneath her sadly water-stained bonnet with its dry but still drooping feather. They were the picture of guilt and scandal.

Of all the people she had wished to avoid, Basking was the one she had least expected to meet, thinking him safe in the country. He edged his horse over beside them, and Brookmere was obliged to stop the curricle.

"How delightful to see you so quickly recovered from your sudden fever, my dear cousin." He flashed a smile of pure enjoyment. "It was so sad to hear that you had to miss the ball—really quite a glittering affair, I've heard. But, then, Mrs. Wentworth will already have told you what a success it was." He ran long, snuff-stained fingers through the snowy folds at his neck and sighed. "So sad, too, that dear Aunt Henrietta was called away so inopportunely. And I suppose Lord Norton felt he could not bear to enjoy himself without her, and so stayed at home. I hear they are positively inseparable lately."

Alyssa was at a loss to respond to this malevolent banter. She did not know how Henry Basking had guessed what had happened yesterday, but he had. Of course, she realized that the servants, no matter how loyal, could not be trusted not to gossip about the odd goings-on in Green Street. She watched him in sickening fear as he turned to the silently furious viscount.

"My lord, I hear that you were also unable to appear at the ball last night." Basking snickered. "Quite an epidemic of absences! And yet, how fortunate that you and my dear cousin are well enough to take a lovely drive today."

Brookmere, unable to control himself any longer, uttered a string of oaths that made Alyssa's ears burn. "Get out of my way," he added explosively. "Before I use my whip on you." He had not so much as raised it, when Basking kicked his mount and thundered away.

By now Alyssa had lost all hope, and scarcely noticed when Brookmere nodded stiffly to another couple who drove past them calling a greeting, and forgot to wave back when two young ladies of her acquaintance strolled by. She ignored their raised eyebrows and whispers, but Brookmere's jaw was clenched. She wanted to tell him that it did not matter, that it was too late to pretend to anyone. It would be all over town by the morrow.

It was a very subdued young woman that Lord Brookmere delivered to her stepmother. Hearing the carriage, Clara stopped pacing the front sitting room and, after a peep out the window, ran down the stairs, burst out of the front door and pulled Alyssa into her arms.

"Oh, Clara!" was the muffled cry against her shoulder.

"Whatever has happened? Where are Henrietta and Lord Robert?" She glanced at Brookmere's drawn face and Alyssa's tearstained one. "Can it be possible that you did not find them?" she asked, hurrying them into the house.

Alyssa controlled her tears long enough to explain what had happened, and learning of their accident and their stay at the inn, a stunned Clara sank into the nearest chair. "Then last night you—oh, my dear, and not even your abigail with you!"

Brookmere stepped forward immediately. "Mrs. Wentworth," he said in surprisingly gentle tones. "Before we left on this mad chase I assured you that no harm would come to your stepdaughter. I have kept my word." He shot a glance at Alyssa as if daring her to reveal just what had passed between them at the inn. "However, I am of course planning to do the right thing by Miss Wentworth, and as soon as I have made myself presentable I shall go to place the announcement of our betrothal."

Clara was visibly relieved, but curiously unsatisfied. She had long had her suspicions of why Alyssa had not encouraged any of her suitors and had refused Selbridge's offer. They ought to look happier about it, she thought. But Alyssa ran straight up to her room without even saying goodbye to Lord Brookmere, and it was left to Clara to apologize and thank him for attempting to help.

His lordship shook his head. "No, my dear madam, the apologies should be mine. If it were not for my overconfidence in my driving skill, my poor opinion of Lord Norton's *and* my underestimation of Miss Henrietta's ingenuity..." He paused, and a rueful half smile crossed his face. "I accept full responsibility."

Clara had had a miserable time trying to pretend to enjoy the ball with neither of her fellow hostesses to support her, and was terrified lest the servants begin to spread the true story of the two ladies' absence. She hoped desperately that her glib explanations for the nonappearance of Henrietta and Alyssa would satisfy the curious guests. She had confided in Sir Edward, who had urged her to put her trust in Lord Brookmere.

"With a fellow like Charles on your side, you can be sure it will all come about," he told her. "Ten to one Miss Henrietta is on her way home, dreaming of a big wedding, and Norton is thanking him for rescuing him from his folly."

Now she made her way to Alyssa's room with some trepidation. She had believed Lord Brookmere when he'd assured her that no harm had come to the girl, but at his mention of their engagement, Alyssa had been unable to hold back a sob.

She entered the room softly to find Alyssa lying on her bed, staring dry-eyed at the plaster wreaths on her ceiling. She sat on the edge of the bed and took the stricken girl's cold fingers in hers. "I am so sorry, my dear. It is all my fault. If only I had forbidden you to go with him—"

Alyssa interrupted with a bitter laugh. "How could you have stopped me, Clara? I was so sure I was right.

I believed Lord Brookmere when he said we could overtake them, and we would have, if we had not gotten lost, and then the storm...everything went wrong!''

"And what of this betrothal?" asked Clara timidly.

"It is nonsense," Alyssa murmured, squeezing her eyes shut to fight off renewed tears. "I told him I would deny it. But I can't, can I? I am...trapped."

"But, my love, did you not think what this must mean to you? Your inheritance, Finchwood..."

"Yes, I know, Clara, and I know you will say I ought to be grateful it has turned out this way, but I simply cannot. He cares not a straw for me, and I..." But even to Clara she would not confide her tangled emotions. "I have made him very angry." She closed her eyes again. Clara left her alone, advising her to get some rest before dinner.

It was with a most unpleasant jolt of surprise that after a brief rest and change of clothes, Alyssa found Lord Brookmere sitting with her stepmother in the drawing room. She had not expected to see him again so soon, and she paused in the doorway, afraid to enter, until Clara saw her.

"Do come in, my love. His lordship came to tell us that the announcement will appear tomorrow morning. Since we are about to dine, I have asked him to join us."

Alyssa seated herself beside Clara, and the viscount, who had risen at her entrance, said only, "Good evening," glancing at her almost indifferently. Curiously enough, this gave her courage.

I shall not allow my life to be like this evening, she thought. Years of silent dinners, indifference, loneliness lay ahead . . . he would absent himself and for her there would be nothing but society and sordid little flirtations, the only alternative being to bury herself at Finchwood. She would take steps to change these prospects very soon, she promised herself.

For now, she would assume a placidity that would astonish him. Tomorrow she would send a note to Lord Selbridge.

Clara and Brookmere had been speaking of the betrothal, and they continued to make arrangements in which the prospective bride took no interest. In a few minutes Sir Edward arrived, and he pressed her hand so kindly that she knew he must have been told the story. She was grateful that he was too well-bred to speak of it.

Alyssa managed to get through the meal without having to address a single direct word to her betrothed, but afterward there was no escaping him. He came over to her in the corner of the drawing room where she sat embroidering a chair cover she had begun as a gift for Clara.

"May I sit down?" he inquired, gesturing toward the empty place beside her on the mahogany settee. She bowed her head in acquiescence and did not meet his gaze.

"Miss Wentworth, although this betrothal is not to your liking, it is for your own protection that I must force you to agree to it. I am sure that once word gets out—as it no doubt will, since that Basking creature saw us—that you were not at home in bed with a fever last night, I am sure you will be glad that you have consented to the engagement."

"But it is not in his interest to spread such a rumor," Alyssa could not help pointing out. "You know the facts. If I marry you, he is cut out of the inheritance."

Brookmere nodded. "Yes, and do you think that he will let it happen quietly? If a few days go by and there is no word of our betrothal, he will never be sure that it won't happen eventually. A man of his character might do something...desperate. It is better if he knows immediately that he would have to answer to me first."

It had not occurred to Alyssa that her cousin might do something to prevent the marriage, and she shivered a little at the thought of his greedy eyes on her and his moist lips on her hand. But it did not alter her plans in any way.

"No doubt you are right, my lord," she said with uncharacteristic meekness. "I offer no further objections."

He could not but be surprised at her change of attitude, but the total indifference in her voice did not flatter him that she found him any more acceptable than before. He reached into his pocket, bringing forth a slim red jewel case. "These were my mother's and my grandmother's before her. They are a tradition in the family, to be passed on to the future viscountess on her betrothal."

Alyssa opened the lid and caught her breath, for within were the most beautiful jewels she had ever seen. There was an exquisitely worked necklace of gold, emeralds and diamonds in the design of a flowering vine, a pair of matching earbobs and a ring

with a large perfect emerald surrounded by diamonds.

Brookmere watched as she turned them over in her
hands, her eyes glowing in appreciation. She met his
gaze briefly, but his expression was unfathomable.

"Why don't you put it on?" he suggested, indicat-
ing the ring. She hesitated, but finally slid it onto her
finger.

"They are beautiful," she whispered just loudly
enough for him to hear. He moved closer to admire the
ring on her finger and she shivered at his nearness. He
quickly moved away.

"I am glad you like them," he said matter-of-factly.
"I am arranging a reception for tomorrow evening to
introduce you to some of my friends. If you have no
objection, I would like you to wear them."

She merely nodded and thanked him quietly, secretly assuring herself that the jewels, however lovely,
would not be hers for long. If she could not have the
viscount's love, then his jewels could bring her no
happiness.

The two gentlemen left early, Sir Edward taking a
tender farewell of Clara, while Brookmere only bowed
over his fiancée's hand.

"Whatever your opinion of me, Miss Wentworth," he said "I flatter myself that I am fairly well
regarded in the world. If I introduce you as soon as
possible as my intended wife, what cannot but be regarded as a highly irregular betrothal will be attended
with the minimum of scandal." He paused, as if waiting for her comments, but Alyssa was staring deter-
minedly at the floor, wishing him gone.

"It would be well," he continued, "if we could contrive to be seen together in public tomorrow. If you have no objection, I shall call for you in the afternoon to drive in the park."

She murmured her assent, and at last he was gone. By tomorrow afternoon, she vowed, it would not make an ounce of difference whether anyone saw them in each other's company or not. Back in her room, she penned a delicately worded note to Lord Selbridge. She only hoped, as she put it into the hands of her servant, that he would not think it too presumptuous of her to expect him to come at her call after she had refused his offer.

But she knew he would present himself in Green Street tomorrow morning, and if all went well she might free herself from this tangle, or at least from the pain of seeing that cold indifference in the eyes of the man she loved.

CHAPTER FIFTEEN

SELBRIDGE ARRIVED EARLY the next day. Clara raised her eyebrows but made no objection when Alyssa asked to see him alone. His face wore a bewildered expression, and his voice and manner were uncharacteristically solemn.

"Miss Wentworth, please accept my most sincere wishes for your every happiness. Lord Brookmere is a man for whom I have the greatest respect."

"Why, whatever—oh, the *Morning Post*, to be sure..." she said in confusion.

He looked at her in surprise. "Certainly I have seen the paper, as has everyone else in town. There is no question of a mistake? Are you not betrothed to Lord Brookmere?" His tone was the tiniest bit hopeful.

"Oh, no, there is no mistake—not about the announcement. However..."

He looked at her, imploring to be let in on the mystery. She obliged him by asking him to sit down and began by saying, "I must thank you for your good wishes, and indeed it is extremely kind of you to come here, after..."

He dropped his solemnity at her very real distress. "Please, my dear Miss Wentworth, do not feel badly about refusing me. It was obvious, even then, that there was a rival for your affections, and I would not wish you to feel guilty for following your heart's dictates."

"But it is not like that at all! I must explain."

"Please." Selbridge leaned forward in his chair, his gaze fixed unwaveringly on her face.

"If you will be patient with me, my lord...you see, it is not an easy thing to relate, and I know I can rely on you to keep what I have to say within the walls of this room."

He was all eager attention as she described her aunt's elopement and the events that had followed. His eyes widened in alarm as she told him of the accident, and then, very carefully, she described the night at the inn, explaining that Lord Brookmere had behaved with the utmost circumspection. Her face burned at such a lie, knowing that anyone witnessing those kisses would have considered her compromised, if not ruined.

"You may rely on my discretion, my dear," he assured her as she concluded her embarrassing tale. "But am I given to understand, my dear, that this betrothal, this engagement to Brookmere, is only of necessity?"

She could not meet his eyes, but he took her evasion for modesty. "If I must marry to save my reputation, then I would prefer it to be to a man whom I truly admire and respect, and who I know has my best interests at heart."

The earl could not believe his ears, but incredulity turned swiftly to joy, as her meaning became clear to him.

"Then you will be my wife?"

When she nodded, painfully aware of her grave sin of omission in not informing him that she was in love with Brookmere, she found herself taken in a very gentle embrace and kissed very chastely and briefly, as if she were a porcelain doll, too delicate for more passionate treatment.

"I am so very grateful to you, my lord, for understanding me," she said when he had released her. "I know it is not at all proper for a lady to request a renewal of an offer of marriage. Indeed, it is quite shabby of me to use you in this fashion, when you are so good—" She stopped, for he was looking at her with such tenderness that guilt choked her.

Selbridge assured her that far from feeling ill-used, he considered himself the luckiest man in England.

"The only thing I must ask, my lord, and I terribly regret having to do it, is that we may keep it secret until I am able to convince Lord Brookmere to allow me to cry off. He is very stubborn, and where he feels it to be his duty... Of course I shall accept blame for ending the engagement."

The earl took her hand and brought it to his lips. "I completely understand, my darling. Whenever you are ready, just tell me, and we shall soon fix on the day that will make me the happiest of men."

She managed to suppress her inclination to wince, and even to smile at him. When he asked her if she would like him to speak to Brookmere for her, she hastily declined the offer.

"Oh, no, my lord, it is kind of you, but I must not do it that way. It would be too cowardly of me. It had much better come from me, as he might take offense if I left you to say it. After all, the whole affair was my fault entirely.''

His lordship the earl assented, and after pressing her hand to his lips once more, he left, saying, ''You are an angel, and you have made me very happy.''

When he had gone, Alyssa sagged against the sofa in relief, but it was short-lived, for she did not know how she would convince Brookmere to dissolve the engagement. She had little confidence in her ability to brazen it out and tell him she was in love with Selbridge. One look from those penetrating blue eyes and her bravado would crumble. No doubt he would find it amusing to learn that the cold-blooded heiress was really in love with him.

She hardly had time to ponder all the implications of what she had done, when she was besieged by callers. The announcement of the betrothal had, not unexpectedly, caused much excitement. In response to all the questions, she found it very trying to repeat the details of the supposed secret engagement that Clara and Brookmere had agreed upon to satisfy the world's curiosity. And still there were sly glances and whispers.

Mary had at first been wild with joy for her, but one look at Alyssa's face showed her the misery in those green eyes above the brittle smile. Despite her intention not to reveal the secret, Alyssa found herself confiding in her friend, at least to the extent of telling her how the betrothal had come about.

''But this is not so very bad! Your problem is solved, and I am sure, my dear, that Brookmere, honorable though he is, would not allow an incident like this to tie him to a female for whom he has no affection."

For a moment Alyssa was heartened, but recalling his late behavior to her, she sighed and shook her head. "No, Mary, I fear he has less regard for me than ever. And he is prouder than you can imagine. He insisted on the marriage, no matter what objections I made, especially after my cousin Basking saw us."

Mary gave up attempting to persuade her that her future was, if not a rosy one, at least not as bleak as her imagination painted it. Though Alyssa could not bring herself to reveal everything to her friend, she was grateful for her support, as some of the other callers were not above showing their jealousy. Many were the subtle, but spiteful barbs directed against her by those who did not consider a tradesman's daughter a suitable bride for Lord Brookmere. By the afternoon, Alyssa was exhausted by the strain and much more inclined to collapse on her bed than to keep her engagement to drive with the viscount. But four o'clock saw her seated beside Brookmere in his phaeton, drawn by such a fine pair of grays that, even in her distress, she could not help admiring them.

Thus they eased into a conversation about horses, while the fashionable world stared to see that most elusive and eligible parti, Viscount Brookmere, driving his fiancée about the park. Once more Alyssa had to endure the congratulations and unabashed curiosity of her acquaintances, and she chafed under the restraint of their presence, for she had intended to inform Brookmere of the change in their plans as soon as possible.

When at last they were left to drive on alone, Alyssa searched for a way to open the subject. Just as she thought she had found the words and the courage to do so, she found she could not utter a sound, for riding toward them on a showy chestnut hack was Henry Basking.

His small eyes gleamed with malice even as his lips formed a determined smile, and he brought his horse over to Alyssa's side, avoiding Brookmere. "My apologies, cousin, for not being among the first to offer my congratulations," he said smoothly, noting the viscount's tightened mouth and Alyssa's pale face. "It seems that you have won after all, my dear, and I hope that I shall never hear it said that you won by unfair tactics."

"I doubt if anyone would be so vulgar as to make any such comment," she said acidly, "especially as it is quite a private, family matter. And if you dare to insinuate—"

"Why, I meant nothing by it, coz, and indeed there is nothing at all odd in it—a secret engagement. Quite commonplace." His lips still smiled, but his eyes were full of hatred. "How strange that people are already beginning to whisper..."

"If they are whispering—" Alyssa's eyes were blazing, but she kept her voice low, so as not to be heard by curious passersby "—it is not because there is anything odd about it, but because you put the idea in their heads."

Basking feigned hurt. "You must allow me some small compensation, my dear, for losing my inheritance..."

"I'll allow you five seconds to take yourself off before I get down from this carriage and show you just what I think of your meddling," said Brookmere in a voice edged with steel.

Basking laughed, but moved away, his glance passing warily from Alyssa to Brookmere. "The bold defender of the helpless maiden! Very well, I shall leave you lovebirds to each other—for now."

He rode away, and Alyssa was ashamed to find that she was trembling. "Oh, he knows the truth, and even though we are engaged, he is still going to spread rumors!" Her crying off from the engagement now would cause twice as much of a stir if Basking told everyone his tale. How could she drag Selbridge into such a scandal?

Brookmere's eye glittered dangerously. "If he threatens you again," he said through clenched teeth, "let me know immediately and I shall deal with him."

Alyssa thought she had never seen him so angry, even when she had argued with him at the inn, and stared at him, amazed. But he laughed at the look on her face.

"It's not such a tragedy, my dear. I only hope that you are satisfied at last of where it would lead if we did not go through with this marriage. Oh, don't think I was fooled by your sudden capitulation," he said, and she looked away, feeling foolish. "It's not in you to give up so easily. But bear in mind that if Basking had his way, everyone in London would know the truth about our adventure."

"But then he would be no better off than he is now, for he would still lose the inheritance."

"Unless you could be induced to marry him instead of me." Brookmere gazed, unconcerned, over the horses' heads.

"Never!" she cried, and then promptly turned pink under his amused sideways glance.

"I am flattered," he said wryly, "that I do not rate so low in your estimation as to make a marriage with your cousin preferable."

Now was certainly not the time, she decided, to inform him that it was Selbridge she preferred to marry. Her courage had dissolved. It would be even more difficult to do it after he had formally introduced her as his fiancée, but though she might be made to figure as a jilt, his own consequence would not suffer for long. So she allowed him to hand her down from the phaeton and bade him farewell until the evening, with only a twinge of guilt at her cowardice.

WHEN ALYSSA, attired in gold net over white satin and adorned with the viscount's jewels, arrived at the Brookmere town house in Mount Street, she was impressed in spite of herself with the size and elegance of the house. Brookmere seemed pleased with her reaction.

"Do you like it?" he asked almost shyly. "If there is anything you wish to change once we are married, just tell me and it shall be done. The house has not been redecorated in years and most of these things should no doubt be retired to the attics by now. I shall leave it to your discretion."

Alyssa was almost ashamed at this show of confidence, but composed herself to meet his lordship's friends. His brother, he informed her, was at present on his wedding trip in Italy, while his mother, who suffered from indifferent health and spent most of the year in Bath, could not make the journey to London. "I shall take you to see her," he promised. "Of course I have written by messenger to inform her of our engagement."

Deeper and deeper still, thought Alyssa. However would she extricate herself? The viscount seemed to regard the idea of their marriage with amazing complacency, considering that he was just as trapped as she. No doubt, though, in time-honored fashion, marriage would interfere not one bit with any of his accustomed pleasures. She recalled the sight of him driving with that very obvious courtesan, and it stiffened her resolve to end the betrothal.

To her surprise, many of the most respected names in society, some of whom she had never managed to meet, appeared in Mount Street to pay their respects to her as the future Viscountess Brookmere. Though outwardly calm, she squirmed inwardly under the scrutiny of imposing dowagers and gentlemen of impeccable lineage. She had just recaptured her hand from that of an aged but still gallant peer, when she looked up to see Lord Selbridge approaching, a severe-looking dowager on his arm.

She threw a startled glance at Brookmere, who murmured that the countess was one of his mother's close friends. The countess nodded frostily as Alyssa curtsied to this stern matriarch. She was warmer to Brookmere, but very obviously she, like some others, was not pleased with the viscount's choice. What she would say if she knew her son's plans did not bear contemplating, and Alyssa dreaded the thought of such a mother-in-law.

Selbridge only bowed over her hand and smiled, after giving polite, if uneffusive congratulations to Brookmere. He raised an eyebrow in question at Alyssa and she shook her head slightly. His face fell, and he had to be prodded away from the receiving line by his mother's ebony walking stick.

Brookmere left her side to confer with his butler, and Lady Pomeroy, looking quite satisfied, descended on her great-niece. She pinched her cheek and congratulated her on her success.

"What did I tell you, gel? I was right all along, wasn't I? Of course I can't take all the credit for it," she admitted. "As that silly aunt of yours would say, it was all owing to true love, eh?"

Alyssa managed a wan smile.

"What's this, still not happy?" Lady Elizabeth looked at her searchingly. "Don't tell me the fool has quarreled with you!"

She hastily assured her great-aunt that nothing of the sort had occurred.

"Hmmph," said her ladyship and would have said more had not the earl arrived at Alyssa's elbow. The baroness wandered off to find her cronies.

"My darling," he whispered. "I beg of you, if you are to tell Brookmere, do it soon. You cannot know how it tears at my heart to have everyone think that—"

"Please, my lord!" Alyssa was terrified that someone would hear him. "I should not wish to rouse any suspicions."

"I am sorry." He schooled his features into a less fervent expression. "But if you have any affection for me at all, do it soon," he begged softly.

It was impossible to attempt to explain how difficult was her task, but she promised that she would try to speak to Brookmere alone by the end of the evening, and with this he had to be content.

A supper followed, of which Alyssa in her anxiety could eat scarcely a bite. Several times she saw Brookmere looking at her curiously, and she noted that the earl watched them both in a manner that would appear very singular to anyone who was at all prone to suspicion.

Thankfully, both the ladies and gentlemen retired to the drawing room together, for Alyssa dreaded being left to the mercy of the ladies and their stiff, polite conversation and veiled questions. Some of the viscount's younger friends were kinder, and she began at last to relax in their company.

But when Brookmere came to join them, they all smiled knowingly and scattered, leaving the affianced couple alone. She felt Selbridge's eyes on them from across the room, and gathered her courage for what she must do.

"How do you like my friends, Miss Wentworth?" The viscount asked, smiling down at her in a way that caused her even more pain.

She saw the line she must take. "The question you ought to ask yourself, my lord, is how do your friends like me? Not very much, I would think. The daughter of a tradesman is not a fitting match for a name as old and distinguished as yours."

"That is my concern, not yours." His voice was cool.

"Why are you so stubborn? Can't you see that it simply won't work?" she pleaded. Finally he really looked at her, and she wanted very badly to become lost in his eyes and throw her arms around him, anything but do what had to be done.

"What are you trying to say, Alyssa?" He had never used her first name before, and the sound of it on his lips made her want to weep, but she had no choice.

"I'm trying to say that I—that we cannot—" Her distress was so great she did not realize she was staring helplessly, anywhere but at Brookmere's grim face.

Selbridge was watching, saw the panic in her eyes, and could restrain himself no longer. He left his seat and came immediately to her side.

"What has happened, my dear? Will you not let me—"

"No, it is nothing, n-nothing at all," she stammered, feeling the viscount's incredulous gaze on them.

A light had gone out of Brookmere's eyes, a light she had never noticed before. "Please excuse my antiquated notions, my lord," he said to Selbridge with icy politeness, "but if my fiancée is in distress I am sure I am quite capable of attending to her without any assistance."

The earl started guiltily, for he knew himself to be, at least in the eyes of the world, a trespasser. But he had no stomach to continue the pretense any longer.

"I'm sorry, Brookmere, but perhaps I should explain—"

Alyssa cut him short. "No, my lord please, I will explain to Lord Brookmere. Please leave us, and I will tell him everything." Her look compelled him to obey. He pressed her hand once and, with a short bow, strode away.

This was not at all how she had intended to do it, but by now Alyssa was eager to have done with the horrid scene. She braced herself to meet the viscount's gaze again, and the anger that blazed there startled her, until she considered what a blow this must be to his pride.

"Miss Wentworth," he said coldly, "I will thank you, in future, not to embarrass me in my own home." He glared after the retreating figure of the earl and Alyssa shrank from his anger.

"Now I take it there is something you wish to say to me."

"Yes," she said expressionlessly, avoiding his eyes. "I—I am not going to marry you." She heard his sharp intake of breath, but when she looked up his face was rigid. "This travesty of a betrothal is no longer necessary. There is a gentleman whose offer of marriage I had once refused and whom I now . . . who would still . . . who I would prefer . . ." Try as she might, she could not say that she loved Selbridge.

"I am going to marry Lord Selbridge." She didn't even realize she was sliding the emerald from her finger until Brookmere stopped her.

"It is hardly necessary to strip yourself of the jewels here before my guests," he said woodenly. "You may send them to me tomorrow. I am sorry if my insistence on this engagement has caused you any difficulties with Selbridge. He is a good man, and I cannot do other than hope he will make you happy. In any case, the purpose is served. Your good name is safe in his hands. I wish you well.''

Alyssa, with her heart in her throat, noted his calm acceptance and came to the conclusion that she had done the right thing. This was not a man who was devastated by her news. He was certainly surprised, but the glibness with which he uttered these banalities was proof of his indifference.

''Though I was attempting to preserve your reputation, I realize that by the liberties I have twice taken with you, I have done more to jeopardize it than anyone. I most sincerely apologize. It was . . . ungentlemanly of me.''

The memory of those kisses burst over her like a sheet of flame, and she struggled to keep her composure. She was nothing to him. How else could he, she wondered, appear so cool and unaffected, while she ached with such a terrible regret?

''I'm sorry,'' she whispered, staring down at her hands clenched in her lap, watching as the emerald on her finger reflected the candlelight in its depths. She unclenched her hands and rose from her chair.

''Yes,'' said the viscount softly, ''so am I.''

CHAPTER SIXTEEN

"MY DEARS!" cried Henrietta, hugging Clara and Alyssa repeatedly, tears of joy streaming down her plump cheeks. "It was the most wonderful thing imaginable, such a wedding, so romantic in every particular!"

The day following Lord Brookmere's reception had brought the long-awaited arrival of Lord and Lady Norton from their unconventional wedding journey. Henrietta was triumphant, and her new husband no longer wore his customary expression of melancholy, but rather a look of stunned surprise.

Even Alyssa, who throughout the day had appeared to be in a waking dream, had revived enough to smile at the sight of Lord Norton's blush as his new wife blew a kiss to him. She sat quietly beside Clara as Henrietta burst into apologies and explanations.

"I know you both would have wanted to see me married, but it was simply insupportable! Miss Norton was on her high ropes again, and this time even dear Robert could say nothing to persuade her. She was horrid enough to say that she would bar the door to the house rather than have me supplant her as its mistress!" Lady Norton's eyes flashed with indignation, and her husband stirred uneasily in his chair.

"Now his lordship and I are going to march straight there and present her with a *fait accompli,* are we not, my dear?" She smiled sweetly at Lord Norton, who did not look at all up to dealing with the fracas that would undoubtedly ensue. Clara took pity on him and offered brandy, which he accepted gratefully.

Henrietta had heard nothing of the pursuit that had trailed her, or of its disastrous consequences. Her mouth fell open in amazement when Alyssa told her the story, for she had never expected such a result from her hasty flight.

"Oh, my poor dear niece," she cried. "I never thought you would try to stop me. Why, what would anyone have cared? Besides, it was too romantic to be improper! How daring of you, poor child, all alone with a gentleman...."

She fumbled for her handkerchief and Lord Norton, with the air of one who has had much practice, came to her aid with his own.

"And the chaise overturned? You were not injured?"

"Not a bit," her niece assured her. "I am sorry to say, aunt," she continued with the ghost of a smile, "that the only thing in danger of being injured was my reputation, except that Lord Brookmere, immediately we knew our situation, proposed marriage."

Henrietta snapped to attention, leaving off her crying at this interesting turn of events. "Why, then you are betrothed to Lord Brookmere! That is marvelous news! All our worries about Henry Basking and Finchwood are quite over!" She was now in such transports of joy as to make her previous bout of tears tame by comparison.

Both Alyssa and Clara cautioned her that, to allay suspicion, it was being put about that there had been a secret engagement. They also made her aware of the excuses made for her own and Alyssa's absence from the ball, at which she lapsed into fresh apologies.

"Oh, Clara, I hope it was not quite ruined. No one has suspected the truth?"

"Not yet," Alyssa told her. "But now that you are back and married, no one is going to believe that you were in Bath with a sick friend, and Henry Basking has let me know that he had his suspicions about what really happened. He is quite furious enough to spread any rumor if he thought it would do him any good." She stopped, shrugged and smiled faintly. "It will not signify now, I suppose, whatever he may choose to tell people. He can do nothing about it, and once I am married, the talk will die away." Clara and her sister-in-law exchanged a worried glance. Alyssa's eyes had lost their sparkle, her skin its translucence, and even her lips were pale. Clara had not dared to question her, but it was obvious that something of moment had occurred last evening, of which she did not care to speak.

Alyssa knew she ought to announce the breaking of one betrothal and the formation of another, but every time she intended to speak, something prevented the words from leaving her lips. Even the night before, she had kept up the show for the benefit of the guests, though her heart was breaking and Brookmere's manner was brittle. Fortunately Selbridge had soon slipped away quietly, with the excuse that his mother was fatigued. She shuddered to think of that haughty lady's reaction to his announcement.

After wishing her aunt and new uncle good fortune in dethroning Miss Norton, and declining Clara's suggestion that they begin shopping for wedding clothes, Alyssa retired to her room. She forced herself to sit down and begin a note to accompany the return of the jewels to Brookmere, but several attempts left her only with a pile of crumpled paper. She gave it up, and, after packing the jewels away in their case, was about to ring for a footman to take them to Mount Street, when Nan knocked briefly and entered, bearing a sealed note. "Mr. Oliver says a servant brought this and is waiting for a reply."

The letter was written in a strong, spiky hand that she did not recognize. To her surprise it was from her Great-Aunt Elizabeth, who demanded her presence in Portman Square immediately, adding that she had sent her own carriage for Alyssa, and that she should lose no time.

Though it was entirely in character, Alyssa could not help but be puzzled by this summons, and wondered why Lady Pomeroy had troubled to send her own carriage. Nevertheless, after perusing the note again, Alyssa glanced out the window at the scudding clouds, saw leaves from the trees in the nearby square being blown about the house tops and quickly changed her clothes for more suitable outdoor wear.

It would not do to keep her great-aunt waiting, although she feared that an uncomfortable interrogation, or at least a scold, awaited her. Had she somehow learned of the betrothal to Selbridge? Luckily, he was one of the old lady's favorites, so perhaps she would be lenient.

When she went down, Alyssa had a momentary qualm, for the carriage that awaited her was attended by a couple of burly fellows who looked more like prizefighters than footmen. The coachman, too, was so unlike her aunt's almost uniformly elderly servants that she was taken aback. But she told herself that her nerves were overset by her recent difficulties. The men wore red-and-gold livery, the Pomeroy colors, so that it was foolish of her to be wary of them.

"Please to hurry, miss," said the footman gruffly as she stood considering the carriage, "'Er ladyship said right away."

His manner decided her. "I am waiting for my maid to bring my pelisse." She reproved him with a glance.

She scolded herself for feeling so inexplicably anxious about her aunt's summons. Nevertheless, when Nan came down with her pelisse and gloves she took the abigail aside, after ordering her own phaeton to be brought round.

"You need not come with me, Nan, for I have decided to drive myself in my phaeton. I am feeling a little unwell, and sitting in a closed carriage would only make it worse."

"But, miss, it isn't proper you should go alone—"

"I shall not be alone," Alyssa said firmly, noting the impatience of the footman, who paced beside the carriage. "I shall have Ned for a groom, and you may stay and mend the rent in my yellow silk dinner gown. I daresay I shall not be gone long." A glance at the darkening sky told her that rain was very likely. A fine fool she would look, arriving in an open carriage, soaked to the skin. But she could not make herself get into the closed vehicle with the strange servants.

An uneasy Nan went back into the house, and though Lady Pomeroy's servant attempted to dissuade her, Alyssa waited until the phaeton was ready. With a sigh of relief, she took the reins in her hands and drove toward Portman Square, her own sturdy groom perched behind her. Lady Elizabeth's servants had said nothing more, but only followed her carriage.

Upon rounding a corner, she saw Mary Carstairs, accompanied by a maid, driving in an open carriage and looking worriedly at the clouds. They stopped only briefly as they passed each other, Alyssa explaining her strange errand. Mary looked suspiciously at the coachman of Lady Pomeroy's carriage.

"It seems very odd to me, but... perhaps it is only one of these fancies that women in my condition often have." The ladies exchanged a rueful glance as the rain began and wet spots began to appear on their muslin skirts.

"Hurry home, my dear, before you are soaked," Alyssa told her, "and don't worry about me."

The two carriages passed and Mary had traveled not a block, when, on impulse, she turned. She was astonished to see Lady Pomeroy's carriage suddenly swing in front of Alyssa's, obstructing its path and, indeed, narrowly missing it. Mary could see the small figure of her friend struggling to control her horses as the carriage rocked and swayed, while the groom leaped down and tried to calm the animals.

She was about to order her coachman to go to their assistance, when to her amazement the door of Lady Pomeroy's carriage was flung open and a thin figure, seeming vaguely familiar, sprang across to Alyssa.

With the assistance of his groom, he wrestled her down from her seat despite her frantic struggles.

"Turn back!" Mary cried, "We must help her!" But by the time they had turned in the narrow street, they were close enough to witness the end of the struggle and too late to do anything for Alyssa. In seconds, she was gagged and bundled into the carriage. Before her groom could intervene, the carriage had thundered away.

Alyssa's groom, as soon as he restored order to the horses and harness, leaped back into the vehicle and shot off after his mistress.

Mary's carriage likewise sprang away at her order. "To Green Street, at once!"

ONCE INSIDE THE CARRIAGE and freed from the grip of the footman, Alyssa tore the cloth from her mouth and flung herself into a corner of the carriage as far as possible from her captor. Facing her on the opposite seat, she was not very surprised to see, was her cousin Henry Basking.

He was panting slightly from his exertions, and his grin chilled her blood. Facing the rear window, she could see her own carriage in pursuit, but growing smaller and smaller as it fell behind, unable to overtake them.

Alyssa struggled to calm the pounding of her heart and, above all, to keep her wits about her. Basking's eyes were gleaming in a most unpleasant way, and when he moved closer, she forced herself not to shrink back, but faced him unflinching, chin up, green eyes flashing fire.

"So, my brave little cousin, even when our great tall viscount is not here to protect us, we can still be defiant, eh?" He reached out a pale hand to her, but she struck it away before it could touch her, repulsion getting the better of her good sense.

Basking only laughed. "Time enough for that, sweeting, when we have reached our destination. After we have been officially made one with the help of this." He waved a paper that could only have been a special license. "My dear mother, when the situation was explained to her, agreed at once that we ought not to put off the marriage, and so a word to her friend the bishop, and it was done."

"You deceive yourself, sir" she replied as coolly as possible. "For you will not take Finchwood and the Wentworth fortune that way. I assure you that I will never marry you."

He laughed again, a sound that made the gooseflesh stand out on her arms.

"Let us not be too hasty, my dear. Perhaps it may take a bit of convincing, but in the end you will agree that it is quite the most sensible thing you could do. Besides, our nuptials shall be attended by only a very select group of my friends, none of whom shall pay any attention to your protests."

The pattering of the rain on the carriage roof was louder now, and glancing out of the window, Alyssa saw that they were almost past the boundaries of London, on a route she did not recognize.

Basking anticipated her next thought. "I should not think of jumping out, sweet coz, as we are traveling at far too great a speed for such acrobatics."

She affected indifference. "I am sure that you have considered the consequences of such a foolish plan," she said contemptuously. "Tell me, how do you intend to defend yourself to Lord Brookmere when he comes to deal with you?"

With a swift movement he was across the carriage and on the seat beside her. Alyssa could smell his sour breath and the sickening odor of his eau de cologne as he leaned over her. "Your former fiancé will have no way of knowing where you are until it is too late. After our marriage, I shall take good care that you remain secluded, and you can be assured that you will never see him again, for if he should prove difficult, we shall simply travel to the continent. Yes, we can live quite nicely there on our fortune."

He put a hand under her chin, while she merely stared at him scornfully. "I regret, my dear, that I do not come to you as such a splendid specimen of masculine perfection as you are accustomed to. However, once I am master of your papa's fortune I shall have no objection to your amusing yourself just as you please. My groom is a stout, vigorous fellow. No doubt he will do well enough. Or shall you search for a *titled* lover?"

The sneer on his face was more than she could bear. It was the work of an instant, but the rage had been building up inside her for so long that Alyssa did not pause to think. She drew back her arm and lunged at Basking, catching him an unpracticed, but nonetheless effective blow on the chin.

Nursing her bruised knuckles, she was at first in too much pain to pay her victim any heed. When he did not retaliate, and instead merely slumped in the seat, she realized she had rendered him unconscious.

Between her amazement and fright, the situation seemed incredibly funny, and Alyssa had to stifle a hysterical laugh lest she alert the servants. But she only heard them cursing the rain. They were unaware that anything was amiss with their master.

Fearing that her cousin would regain consciousness at any moment, and knowing that she would not escape lightly for having made him suffer such an indignity, she thought quickly.

First she struggled to untie his neckcloth without rousing him, and used it to tie his hands behind him. He did not stir, so with more confidence she took the cloth he had used to gag her and forced it between his teeth, tying it firmly about his head. Frantically now, for he was beginning to moan, she tore the bottom flounce from the hem of her gown and used it to tie up his ankles.

Although she did not believe he would stoop to actually harming her, it occurred to her that he might be armed. Sure enough, in the left hand pocket of his coat was a pistol. She knew nothing of weapons, but surmised that the mere sight of it in her hand would have the desired effect. As soon as the carriage slowed, she would jump out and seek assistance. Keeping the pistol trained on Basking, Alyssa sat close to the door and waited.

CHAPTER SEVENTEEN

FOLLOWING AN UNSUCCESSFUL chase after his abducted mistress, Alyssa's groom sped to Green Street to give the alarm. Mary Carstairs had preceded him with the awful news, so after her initial shock Clara was calm enough to question him. He could tell her less than Mary, who was almost positive that the abductor was Henry Basking.

Her mind whirling, Clara heard from a tearful Nan the story of Lady Pomeroy's summons and the strange carriage. Hastily she scribbled a note to the baroness, telling her in a few disjointed phrases what had occurred. Next she sent for Sir Edward, and was abusing herself for not having first of all sent for Brookmere, when to her great relief he appeared.

His lordship had spent a hellish night after the departure of his guests. He had sat at his window steadily consuming the contents of a bottle of French brandy, staring into the moonlight until he was too drunk to resist Mallow's strenuous protests and allowed himself to be put to bed. Although he had awakened a few hours later with a pounding head, one of his valet's foolproof cures soon had him on his feet, and a cold water splash and strong coffee did wonders toward restoring him. His mind, as well as his body was easier, as he had come to a decision during his moonlit binge.

He cursed himself for having been a proud, stubborn fool. The news that Alyssa had engaged herself to marry Selbridge had struck him like an actual physical blow. To the end he had been convinced that once they were married he would be able to change her mind about him. Now he must take action before it was too late.

Thus he was not pleased to find on his arrival at the Wentworth house that the earl was close on his heels, and it was all he could do not to glare at his rival. But the sight of Clara's tearstained face and Mrs. Carstairs's red eyes stopped him from addressing a word to Selbridge.

"Whatever has happened?" inquired the earl as he rushed to Clara's side. "My dear Mrs. Wentworth, everything is at sixes and sevens, the servants rushing about, your housekeeper in hysterics and Miss Wentworth's maid lying in a swoon in the hall!"

Brookmere, intent on his mission, had noticed none of these things and only strode past the distracted Oliver into the sitting room.

"Oh, my lord, thank heaven you are here!" Clara greeted him, too relieved at his arrival to reply to Selbridge. "I was just about to send for you. It is Alyssa. She had been—abducted!"

The ladies poured out the story, and Brookmere's face grew tense. "Basking." He said it softly, but both hands were clenched into fists.

Selbridge gripped his arm. "The blackguard! Where can he have taken her? By God, when I find him I'll—"

Brookmere cut him off. "I agree, but we can do nothing if we don't know where he is." He turned to the ladies. "Do you know anything that might help us, Mrs. Wentworth?"

Clara forced herself to speak through fresh tears. "I—I believe his family home is in Surrey, but that is where his mother lives, and surely he would not take Alyssa there, not if he intended to—"

"You are most likely right," Selbridge agreed, looking grim.

"Does he have a place of his own, a shooting box or some house in the country to which he repairs when town gets too hot for him?" Brookmere asked.

"Yes," cried Mary suddenly," I recall it now. Last year at a house party, Basking turned up one evening—quite uninvited, but that is his way. There was gaming, and I remember some of the gentlemen lost heavily to him. I distinctly recall that some of the wilder young men left with Mr. Basking to spend the rest of the evening at his house, which could not have been far away."

"And the house, Mrs. Carstairs? Where was it?" Selbridge was polite, but his face was taut and his voice shook.

"It was quite near a little town in Hertfordshire called—"

"Dunscombe," said Brookmere, having at last recalled Basking's destination on the day he had confronted him with that shocking list. Shaking off the memory, he turned to the earl. "Do you know where it is?"

"A fine fool I would look if I did not," replied Selbridge. "It is in my own part of the country and I have a house near the next town.'' He slapped his thigh with his riding whip. ''By God, won't this just do for Basking! He'll not dare show his face in London when I finish with him.'' He started for the door.

Before Lord Brookmere could protest that if there were any rescuing to be done, he ought to have a hand in it, a commotion at the door distracted him. A highly indignant Lady Pomeroy descended on poor Clara, Miss Munsen trailing behind.

''Where is the child?'' she demanded. ''Who is the gudgeon who let her go? *I* send for her in such a way? Why, she is not so silly as to believe that I should—'' She stopped, suddenly aware of the presence of Brookmere and Selbridge.

''And what is being done about it?'' She turned on them fiercely. ''You fellows there,'' she said, addressing two of the most respected peers in the land, ''what do you do, standing about here? Why have you not gone after them?''

''Because, my lady, it is only just now that we have discovered where he may have taken her,'' replied the viscount calmly. ''We were just about to leave.''

His look quelled a protest from Selbridge, who soon thought better of refusing the help of a capable man like Brookmere.

Lady Pomeroy was untying the ribbons of her bonnet and had seated herself between the distraught Clara and Mary.

''Well, don't stand there goggling at me then, silly boys, be gone! You young men don't know the meaning of urgency these days. Why, such a thing happened to friend of mine, back in '80, it was,'' she told the ladies, dispatching the two men with a wink and a wave.

They crept out while she was going on with her tale and, once out of the house, flung themselves onto their horses. Not a word passed between them of their unconventional situation, but none was needed. In this pursuit they were of one mind.

The soaking rain had turned the layer of dust on the roads into a slippery mud. Alyssa, still gazing out of the carriage window, was watching the downpour, hoping it would slow the vehicle enough for her to make her escape.

She tried to keep one eye and the pistol on her cousin, who struggled impotently against his bonds, a bruise empurpling his chin. Now fully conscious, he glared at her with eyes full of loathing, and her relief was immense when at last she saw her opportunity.

The vehicle slowed to take a sharp turn onto a fairly broad, but muddy and rutted lane. Gathering her courage, she threw open the door, and after first tossing out the pistol, she leaped onto the road, skirt held high, and landed hard on her feet. There was a stab of pain in her ankle, but she fell to her knees and allowed herself to roll away under a hedge at the side of the lane.

She lay curled up, panting for breath, aware of the ache where she had bruised her knees and elbows by rolling over a protruding root. Her blue gown and pelisse were covered by the mud of the road, but miraculously her bonnet had stayed tied, and it hung wetly down her back by its ribbons. She still had her reticule, but from where she lay she could not see the pistol.

The sound of the carriage faded and Alyssa allowed herself to breathe again. Her mind was busy with plans of begging assistance at the nearest dwelling, and it was with a sudden panic that she discovered she could not put any weight on her right foot. All her attempts to do so caused the most excruciating pain, and she was almost in tears as she sat down again to loosen her half boot, only to find that the ankle was already swollen to twice its normal size. She prodded it gingerly, but could not tell if it had been broken or only sprained.

Searching for a stick to support her, she noted despairingly that the nearest trees were only saplings. She was about to crawl back into the lane in the hope that she could hail a passing traveler for help, when she heard the sound of wheels and felt the vibration of hooves through the ground. Instinctively she ducked back as far from sight as possible, trying to peer out without being seen by the driver. What she saw made her desperate with fear. It was Basking's carriage, returning for her.

He had shown a resourcefulness she had not expected. His servants, having no suspicion of his plight, had continued down the lane, their destination only half a mile away. He had contrived to fall to the floor of the carriage, where by drumming his heels he had succeeded in alerting the men on the box. It was the work of a few moments for them to untie him and return to where he had witnessed his prisoner's escape.

Alyssa watched in horror now as a pair of booted feet strode up and down the lane, only yards away. She lay almost without breathing, trying to stifle a whimper of pain. Her ankle was now throbbing viciously after her attempts to stand. She could have wept when she saw the pistol, which she had long since forgotten, lying only a few steps from Basking, and as he bent to retrieve it, he saw the blue of her dress through its patchy coat of mud.

In a second he was standing over her, pointing the weapon at her with a surprisingly steady hand. "My dear Miss Wentworth, this is not time for such childish games," he said lightly but with more menace than she had ever heard in his voice. "Come out at once and allow me to repay you for the kind turn you did by enlivening an otherwise dull journey with your antics."

"I cannot stand. I've broken my ankle." It was at least partly true.

"How very unfortunate," he said icily. Basking gestured to the groom, and the fellow came to pull Alyssa roughly to her feet. She cried out at the pain and would have fallen, but her cousin ordered curtly, "Hold her up."

He took in her appearance, from her filthy boots and swollen ankle, easily visible after the loss of four inches of flounce, to her muddy face and wet, dangling hair.

"A pity." He shook his head. "You shall have to be more careful of your wardrobe when we are married. Though, to be sure, for serving me such a trick and humiliating me in front of my servants, I ought to shoot you right now." His face was contorted and the hand holding the pistol jerked convulsively. "The fortune will be mine, as it would have been by now but for you."

Alyssa realized he was on the verge of madness and knew that her only hope lay in the chance of someone passing by within the next few moments. She thought wildly of Brookmere, and with searing regret at the choices she had made, all of them wrong. It was impossible, she knew, that he could have any idea of her whereabouts. She pitied poor Clara, who must be prostrate with grief by now.

Finally a gleam of sanity returned to Basking's eyes and he gestured to the groom, who began to half drag, half carry her to the carriage. She was struggling in his grip, when she thought she heard hoofbeats on the road, approaching the lane. She could not tell if it was only her imagination, or perhaps the drumming of the rain still pounding on the carriage roof.

The groom had lifted her practically off the ground when suddenly the sound became unmistakable. She saw her chance. The riders, whoever they were, must be made to turn onto the lane. They would pass very close, only a few yards from where she dangled in the groom's arms.

Basking, as apprehensive as Alyssa was relieved at the approach of the riders, could not help glancing toward the road. In that second, Alyssa cried out for help as loudly as she could and, seeing her cousin distracted, kicked with her uninjured foot at the pistol in his hand. The weapon went off, though she had not dared hope for this, and the report brought a shout from one of the approaching horsemen. Alyssa wriggled out of the servant's grasp and dropped to the ground, endeavoring to spare her ankle the worst of the fall.

Brookmere had been just about to turn off the road onto the lane that led to Dunscombe, when he heard a woman's scream. A second later there was the crack of a pistol and the earl cried, "Hurry, man!" They took the turn almost at a full gallop and thundered down the lane, to find a carriage blocking the way. A slim man stood looking down at a patch of muddied blue at the side of the road, and a husky groom in livery hovered nearby. There was no sign of the weapon, and Brookmere's heart plunged as he looked at the still, blue figure on the ground, until Alyssa struggled to sit up.

"She's all right, heaven be thanked," said Selbridge breathlessly.

"Yes," was all that Brookmere could trust himself to say. "See to him." He indicated the groom, who, having noted the deadly expression on the faces of Alyssa's rescuers, was now trying to make his escape.

Brookmere leaped from the saddle, and in two strides he was upon Basking, whom he felled with one skillful blow. The stocky earl, no stranger to the science of boxing himself, soon had the groom joining his master on the ground. Another moment sufficed to dispatch the footman, who had jumped down from the box to go to Basking's aid. The coachman, apparently finding the odds unsportsmanlike, whipped up the horses and rattled past them, so close that the wheels almost touched the unconscious forms on the road.

Brookmere knelt and scooped an astounded Alyssa into his arms. At the sight of him, she thought she might be dreaming. "You're here," she murmured, and that was all, but she could not take her eyes from his face.

Selbridge witnessed the look that passed between them and saw his dreams of happiness crumbling. He forced himself to speak.

"Let us ride into the town, where we can see to Miss Wentworth. Why don't you take her up with you? Then we shall send someone back to deal with these three." He nodded at the still forms on the ground. His voice was unsteady, his expression sober.

The two men exchanged a long look, but Brookmere said only, "Yes, a very good idea," and lifting Alyssa easily, he set her carefully before him in the saddle.

In spite of her throbbing ankle, she luxuriated in the comfort of his arms, warm and strong about her, and leaned back against his broad chest in contentment, watching his hands, sure and competent, guiding the horse with almost imperceptible movements.

She wanted to tell him how sorry she was and how grateful to him for coming after her. But he had not said a word to her and she told herself she must not read too much into it, that he had only done it out of duty. So all she said was, "I think I have broken my ankle," before the pain became too great and blackness washed over her. Then she felt nothing at all.

CHAPTER EIGHTEEN

THE BLACKNESS WAS RECEDING, and pinpoints of light twinkled beneath her eyelids and teased her until she opened them. Alyssa felt a tightness around her injured ankle, though the agony had subsided to a dull ache. She was lying on a soft, chintz-covered sofa, propped up by pillows, in what appeared to be the parlor of an inn. Through the thin door she could hear the sounds of the taproom, the clinking of tankards and glasses, the rough voices of laborers and heavy footsteps that made the wide floorboards creak.

She was alone, but her muddy pelisse and sodden bonnet had been removed, her stays loosened and her ankle bandaged. As she tried to sit up, the door swung open and a young girl in a long damp apron entered, clucking disapprovingly at Alyssa's attempt to swing her feet off the sofa.

"Now, miss, the apothecary says you're not to try to stand on it yet. Just sit back, and I'll make you comfortable." She rearranged the cushions behind Alyssa's shoulders.

"Where are the two gentleman who brought me here?" she asked anxiously, recalling the events of the day, which seemed now to have happened weeks ago.

"Gentlemen, miss? There was only one gentleman brought you in, unless you mean the one who didn't even stop for a pint of our famous brew, but got straight back on his horse as soon as he saw you safe inside.''

Only one... but which one? Unaware that she had spoken her thought aloud, she was startled when the girl answered promptly, "Why, he that's your betrothed, miss. He said would I call him as soon as you woke up.'' And she was gone.

Her betrothed! Alyssa would have laughed if she were not so suddenly pierced with uncertainty. It could be either one of them. But there was only one man she wanted to see right now. This was her last chance to make everything right, if only he still wanted her.

When the door opened and Lord Brookmere appeared, she was painfully shy of him, after her first flush of joy. She was still afraid that he had come to her not for the reason she hoped, but out of duty and pride. Had she been brave enough to meet his gaze, the look in his eyes as he drew a chair up next to her and took hold of her hand could have told her that she need not have worried.

"Are you all right, my darling?"

Alyssa had never heard his voice so tender, and the sound of those longed-for words broke the spell of her silence.

"Yes, my lord, thanks to you."

"Do try calling me 'Charles,'" he suggested with a smile. "When we are married it will be very tiresome for us to be always 'my lording' and 'my ladying' each other. That is—" he lost some of his assurance as he searched her face "—if you do want to marry me."

The glow on her face and the love in her eyes were answer enough, but her happiness could not be confined and the words rushed out, tumbling over one another in their haste to communicate what she had held inside for so long.

"I have always wanted to marry you, Charles, although perhaps I did not want to admit it, and then when I did know it, I thought you didn't want me, and so when we said those terrible things to each other— oh, will you ever forgive me, my love?—I thought of Selbridge, and so—"

Brookmere stopped grinning to interrupt her by gently covering her lips with his own. It was a brief kiss, but none the less sweet for its short duration.

"This is all quite fascinating, Miss Wentworth," he said, wiping a smudge from her cheek with his handkerchief, "but none of it is at all necessary, because it was my fault alone. Now one thing you said particularly interested me, and it could bear repeating. What was it you called me?" His smile rivaled the glow from the setting sun, which had emerged from behind a cloud to gild the little parlor and its occupants.

"Why," said Alyssa, confused, "I called you 'Charles,' as you asked me...." Suddenly comprehending, she lowered her eyes as a wave of pink suffused her cheeks, and whispered, "'My love.'"

She met his eyes, only to become lost in their azure depths, and he repeated the phrase softly as he traced her lips with a gentle finger.

He drew closer, but she moved first, twining her fingers in his thick brown hair and drawing his head down until their lips met. It was quite some time before they parted, and then only because Alyssa's ankle suddenly gave her a sharp reminder of her recent escapade.

She could not hold back a cry, and he released her immediately. "The wedding will be very soon, I think," he murmured thickly, unable to keep from stroking her neck with his fingertips. Alyssa caught his hand and brought it to her lips. "Yes, please," she said meekly, and then laughed from sheer happiness.

"Enough, my darling, or we shall not make it back to town in time for a celebration supper." He stood up reluctantly and began to help her from the sofa.

"Shall we not be stranded again at an inn together, my lord?" she asked playfully.

"Certainly not, my love. What kind of ramshackle fellow do you take me for?" he replied. "Besides, this place is little more than a tavern, really. They don't lodge travelers here. However," he continued as he began to support her from the room, "there is one particular in which this humble place is far superior to the comfortable old Dove."

"And what might that be, my lord?" inquired Alyssa, admiring the way the waning light turned his eyes to sapphires.

"They *do* have carriages for hire," he said proudly.

Take 4 best-selling love stories FREE
Plus get a FREE surprise gift!

**For the millions who can't read
Give the Gift of Literacy**

One out of five adults in North America
cannot read or write well enough
to fill out a job application
or understand the directions on a bottle of medicine.

**You can change all this by joining the fight
against illiteracy.**

For more information write to:
Contact, Box 81826, Lincoln, Neb. 68501
In the United States, call toll free: 800-228-3225

**The only degree you need
is a degree of caring**

LIT—A—1